Erin

By Carol Martin

© 2026 Phillip Stephens
Corporate Publishing
Published under the pen name Carol Martin
All rights reserved.

No part of this publication may be reproduced, distributed, or transmitted in any form or by any means without prior written permission of the author.

This is a work of fiction. Names, characters, places, and incidents are either the product of the author's imagination or used fictitiously.

ISBN: 978-0-9747108-5-3
First Edition

This novel is an original work of human authorship. Portions of this manuscript were developed with the assistance of artificial intelligence tools for drafting, editing, and refinement in accordance with industry best practices. Final content reflects the author's voice and editorial control.

This novel contains mature themes and language intended for adult readers

Dedication

For the women who endure more than they reveal –
And choose grace anyway.

About This Story

This is a story about the lives we live and the ones we keep hidden.

It is about the quiet decisions that shape us, the assumptions that define us, and the moments that change everything before we fully understand why.

Erin is not a single story. She is, in many ways, a reflection of the contradictions we all carry: strength and vulnerability, truth and concealment, survival and grace.

Some choices are made for us. Others we make in silence.
And sometimes, what appears to be coincidence is something far more deliberate though we may only recognize it in hindsight.

This story does not offer easy answers.

It simply asks you to look a little closer, judge a little less and leave room for grace.

Epigraph

There are no coincidences.
Only moments we don't understand yet.

Chapter One

If the world insisted on seeing her as fallen, there was a strange freedom in letting them believe it. – Erin

The first time Erin Carter was called a whore, she was sixteen.

She remembered the weight of the word landing like a physical blow. She hadn't even kissed the boy sitting on the couch beside her. In truth, she had been too shy to try. That made the accusation sting even more.

The slur had come from her mother, hissed across the living room with drunken certainty. It hung over Erin afterward like a dark cloud, coloring every glance and conversation with suspicion. She had already been afraid to bring the boy home, knowing her mother could be volatile and her father might already be drunk.

Now, nearly ten years later, Erin stood in a hotel bathroom adjusting a blonde wig before walking into a stranger's room.

She barely recognized the woman in the mirror.

"Misty."

The name belonged to someone else entirely. A manufactured woman with golden hair, confident eyes, and a practiced smile. Erin tugged at a loose curl of the wig, remembering the whispers that had followed her through high school hallways after her mother's accusation.

For years the label had clung to her like smoke. Eventually the thought had settled in her mind like a bitter seed: if the world insisted on seeing her as fallen, there was a strange freedom in letting them believe it.

But only for now.

Only until she finished school.

Erin inhaled slowly, steadying the churn of nerves in her chest. The familiar mask of Misty felt heavier tonight, a role she had learned to play with convincing ease but never without discomfort.

The wig's synthetic strands were cool beneath her fingers. Every time she wore it, the distance between who she was and who she pretended to be felt both comforting and unsettling.

She looked at herself one last time.

The mirror reflected Misty: blonde, confident, inviting. A carefully crafted illusion designed to shield Erin from the world's judgment.

For a moment she searched the reflection for the girl she used to be.

The girl she still believed she was.

The girl who would someday stand in a courtroom and fight for justice.

Erin straightened her posture.

Only a few more encounters. Only a little more money. Then this chapter of her life would be over forever.

She opened the bathroom door and stepped into the quiet hallway.

The plush hotel carpet softened her footsteps as she moved toward the assigned room number. She smoothed the crimson dress hugging her frame, the hem ending mid-thigh and sending a shiver across exposed skin beneath the dim amber lighting.

The neckline plunged far lower than anything in her law school wardrobe, transforming her normally studious appearance into something deliberately enticing, a costume as false as the blonde waves framing her face.

She stopped at Room 714.

For a moment she sensed movement behind one of the nearby doors.

Watching.

Erin knocked.

She rolled her shoulders back, becoming Misty, the confident blonde fantasy.

The door swung open.

A man stood there wearing dark-rimmed glasses and a rumpled dress shirt, his brow already creased in confusion.

"May I help you?" he asked, one hand still gripping the doorknob.

"Are you Dan?" Erin asked softly, aware of eyes somewhere in the hallway.

"Yes."

"I'm Misty."

His frown deepened.

"I'm sorry," he said slowly. "I don't know any Misty."

"Well," she replied, leaning slightly closer, "someone called for me to meet Dan Harper in room 714."

"I didn't call for anyone."

That was unusual. Most men tried to pull her inside before the door even finished opening.

Behind her, a door cracked open in the hallway.

Her skin prickled.

"Someone's watching us," she whispered. "Could I please come in? It's… not safe out here."

Dan glanced past her shoulder as another door creaked.

With visible reluctance, he stepped aside.

Erin slipped into the room, a streak of red against the beige walls and navy curtains. The door closed with a quiet click behind them.

His eyebrows knit together.

"I think there's been some misunderstanding," Dan said, pushing his glasses up his nose.

Erin scanned the room quickly, the untouched bed, the open laptop on the desk, conference materials spread across the table.

She placed a hand lightly against his chest.

"Someone thinks you want company tonight."

Dan gently removed her hand.

"They thought wrong," he said calmly. "Do you need me to call someone for you? A cab?"

Something about his expression made her pause.

No hunger.

No entitlement.

Just concern.

"You really have no idea why I'm here, do you?"

"No," he said. "You mentioned feeling unsafe outside. I can call security, or—"

"That won't be necessary." She shook her head then glanced at her watch. "I've got transportation coming later. I'll wait downstairs at the coffee shop. Clearly someone's idea of a joke."

She turned toward the door.

"Wait," Dan said.

She stopped.

"Who sent you here?" he asked. "And how do you know my name?"

Chapter Two

Her grandmother used to say there were no such things as coincidences. Only meetings arranged by God. - Erin

Dan closed the door and followed Erin into the room.

"So," he said cautiously, "who sent you? And how do you know my name?"

Erin felt his eyes on her, but her attention drifted to a desk across the room.

Papers were spread across its surface in loose stacks. Titles jumped out at her, family law, social work, counseling, mandated reporting. Subjects that lived at the intersection of broken homes and the legal system.

Her curiosity stirred immediately.

The room hummed with quiet tension.

Dan ran a hand through his hair, watching her scan the papers.

"You said your name is… Misty?"

"Yes," Erin replied.

She didn't look back at him. Instead, she studied the documents, mentally sorting through what she recognized. Her eyes moved quickly, searching the titles the way a miner searches gravel for a fleck of gold.

Dan shifted awkwardly behind her, clearly unsure where to look or what to say.

"Are you a lawyer?" Erin asked suddenly, glancing over her shoulder.

Her voice was soft, curious.

Dan blinked.

"No. I mean—no." He pushed his glasses up his nose. "I'm a social worker. Just a social worker. I'm here with some coworkers for a conference."

He scratched his head, thinking.

"Wait… did they send you here? I wouldn't put that past them."

Erin folded her arms and studied him.

The tension in the room thickened.

She knew this moment well. As Misty, she held a kind of quiet power over men, an uncomfortable mix of curiosity, temptation, and embarrassment. It was a power she never expected to enjoy, and yet sometimes she did.

After a moment she straightened slightly.

"Someone paid for a couple of hours," Erin said flatly.

The words landed like a dropped coin.

Dan's eyes widened.

"I—I'm married," he said quickly.

His voice carried equal parts surprise and alarm. He gestured vaguely toward the papers on his desk, as if they might shield him.

"I actually need to go over those before tomorrow's conference."

Erin watched him carefully.

His eyes darted around the room, avoiding hers. He looked less like a guilty man and more like someone trapped in a situation he didn't understand.

Like a rabbit caught in a snare.

A flicker of pity tugged at her chest.

The papers on the desk suddenly seemed far less interesting.

"Well… we could have coffee," Erin offered.

"No," Dan said quickly. "You really have to go."

He reached out instinctively to guide her toward the door, then stopped himself halfway, clearly unsure whether touching her would make the situation worse.

Erin noticed.

"What?" she said lightly. "You're not going to let your friends have their tasteless fun?"

"Did you not hear me?" Dan replied, frustration creeping into his voice. "I'm happily married."

"Fine."

She gave a small, understanding smile.

Then she nodded toward the desk again.

"You must run into situations involving kids in toxic environments," she said. "I saw that paper over there, something about due diligence investigating abuse claims."

Dan frowned.

"What?"

Her question clearly caught him off guard.

"Do you work in the city?" Erin continued, her tone casual but her eyes sharp.

Dan hesitated.

"Yes," he said slowly. "Child exploitation cases, actually. Why?"

Erin held his gaze.

For a moment she weighed the strange coincidence of it all. Her grandmother used to say there were no such things as coincidences. Only meetings arranged by God.

Erin studied Dan's eyes, searching for something; honesty, maybe. Or kindness.

"Whoever sent me here must think this is hilarious," she said finally. "You seem like a pretty straight-laced guy."

Dan gave a faint shrug.

"Yeah," he admitted. "I guess I am."

Erin shifted her weight.

"Look… someone paid for two hours," she said quietly. "I'd rather not be standing in the hallway explaining this to your coworkers." Her eyes flicked again toward the desk. "But it would probably be best if I go."

Dan followed her gaze to the scattered papers and then back to her.

"You'd be surprised what passes for humor at these conferences," he muttered.

Erin tilted her head toward the desk again.

"Family law. Child services protocols. Mandated reporting. Interesting conference topics."

Dan nodded toward the papers.

"You read that fast."

"I read titles fast."

Silence settled between them.

Finally, Erin shrugged.

"Well," she said casually, "someone paid for two hours."

Dan blinked.

"I'm not suggesting anything inappropriate," she added quickly. "But if your friends are watching the hallway, it might be easier if I don't leave right away. We could just talk."

Dan considered this.

After a moment he sighed.

"Coffee?" Erin suggested.

He hesitated.

Then he gestured toward the small sitting area.

"Fine. Coffee."

She sat.

Chapter Three

If she learned anything in law school it was that they don't teach you everything in law school. - Erin

Dan set the coffee on the small table between them and lowered himself into the chair opposite her. The hotel-issue ceramic mug clinked softly against the table. The faux leather chair creaked under his weight, the sound breaking the silence that had settled over the room.

Erin wrapped both hands around her cup. Her polished nails caught the light against the white ceramic as the heat seeped slowly into her palms. She watched the thin ribbon of steam drift upward, her eyes distant beneath mascara that had begun to smudge faintly at the corners.

For a moment neither of them spoke.

Then she looked up.

"So you deal with kids in bad situations?"

Dan studied her for a moment before answering.

"Sometimes," he said carefully. "Why?"

Erin gave a small shrug that didn't quite reach her shoulders.

"The papers on your desk. Mandated reporting. Abuse investigations."

Dan leaned back slightly in his chair.

"That's part of the job."

Erin traced the rim of the cup with her thumb. "What happens," she asked, "if someone knows a kid is in a bad home… but there's nothing you can prove?"

Dan let out a slow breath.

"That's one of the hardest parts of social work." He leaned forward, resting his elbows on his knees. "Most people think we can just walk into a house and remove a child if something feels wrong. But it doesn't work that way."

"Why not?"

"Because the law requires evidence," he said gently. "Family courts don't act on instincts. They act on documentation."

Erin frowned slightly.

Her mind flashed back to law school; casebooks, lectures, theoretical arguments about due process and parental rights. Everything had sounded clean and logical in the classroom.

But real life never was. If she learned anything in law school it was that they don't teach you everything in law school.

"So if a kid says nothing… and there are no bruises…"

"Then it becomes complicated." Dan took a sip of coffee.

"Physical abuse is easier to prove. Injuries. Medical records. Witnesses. But emotional abuse? Psychological manipulation? That's harder."

Erin looked down at the floor for a moment.

"What do you mean? I mean… do you see a lot of cases that aren't textbook physical abuse?"

Dan thought for a moment. "You can walk into a house that looks perfect," he said slowly. "Clean kitchen. Family photos on the wall. Parents polite as Sunday school teachers."

He paused.

"But the kid sitting at the table looks like they're waiting for something bad to happen."

Erin's fingers tightened around the cup.

"And that's not enough?"

"No," Dan said quietly. "Not by itself."

He nodded toward the stack of conference papers behind him.

"The court needs patterns. Reports from teachers. Medical professionals. Neighbors. Documented incidents. Something that shows ongoing harm."

"And if the parents are careful?" Erin asked.

Dan glanced at her.

"Careful how?"

"Careful enough to hide it."

A small, knowing smile touched Dan's face. "That happens more often than people think."

Erin leaned forward slightly now, her voice quieter. "What if the kid won't talk? Or… maybe they're just waiting for someone to rescue them?"

"That happens too."

"Why?"

Dan rested his forearms on his knees.

"Kids are loyal," he said. "Even when they shouldn't be."

He stirred his coffee slowly. "Some think they'll get their parents in trouble if they tell the truth. Some are afraid things will get worse if they say anything. And some just think what they're living with is normal."

Erin stared down into the coffee.

"And some think the system is never going to save them," she said softly.

Dan frowned slightly, sensing the weight behind the words, but he let the silence sit between them.

"What if someone else sees it?" she asked.

"A teacher? Neighbor? Relative?"

"Someone close."

Dan nodded. "They can report it."

"And then what? What if they already have and nothing's been done?"

"We investigate," Dan said. "And if we don't find enough, we keep investigating. We watch."

"And if the house is clean? If the parents behave while you're there?"

Dan gave a small shrug.

"Then we keep watching."

"That's it?"

"For a while."

The words lingered in the room.

Erin leaned back slowly.

"And time just keeps ticking," she said. "That sounds a lot like waiting."

"Sometimes it is," Dan admitted.

"And if the kid is stuck there the whole time?"

Dan looked at her again.

This time his expression softened.

"The system isn't perfect," he said. "But it's designed that way for a reason."

"What reason?"

"Because removing a child from a family is one of the most powerful things the government can do."

He leaned back in his chair.

"If we remove kids too easily, we destroy families that could have been fixed."

"Some families can't be fixed."

Dan held her gaze.

"And if you wait too long?" she added quietly, trying to soften her tone.

"Then we fail the child."

Neither of them spoke for a moment.

Finally Erin asked,

"So what would you tell someone who was worried about a kid in that situation?"

Dan didn't ask whose child she meant.

He had already begun to suspect the question wasn't hypothetical.

"I'd tell them to pay attention," he said. "And to keep pressing."

"Pressing who?"

"Teachers. School counselors. Doctors. Social workers."

He paused.

"Write things down. Dates. Incidents. Behavior changes." He tapped the table lightly.

"Eventually patterns become evidence."

Erin nodded slowly.

"And if the system still doesn't move?"

Dan took another sip of coffee.

"Then you keep pushing."

"Why?"

A faint smile crossed his face.

"Because sometimes it works."

Erin studied him. "And when it doesn't?"

Dan's voice softened.

"Then you keep trying until it does."

The room fell quiet again.

Erin looked down into the coffee cup in her hands, her thoughts drifting somewhere far away.

The silence stretched between them.

Down the hallway came the sudden grinding rumble of the hotel ice machine dumping a fresh load into its metal bin. A moment later came the hollow clatter of someone scooping ice into a plastic bucket.

The ordinary noise felt oddly loud after the weight of their conversation.

Dan leaned back in his chair and studied her for a moment. "You ask a lot of questions," he said.

Erin lifted her eyes.

"And you seem pretty smart."

She raised an eyebrow.

"Pretty smart for a prostitute?" she said dryly.

Dan blinked.

"That's not what I meant."

"It's usually what people mean."

"I didn't say that."

"You didn't have to."

Another scoop of ice rattled down the hallway.

Dan rubbed the back of his neck.

"Well," he said slowly, "for someone who reads titles fast, you ask the kind of questions people ask when they already understand the system."

Erin looked down at the coffee again.

"Or understand a failed system. Maybe I just watch people."

"That's part of intelligence," Dan said.

She gave a faint smile.

"Or survival."

Dan nodded. "That too."

The ice machine hummed again before falling silent.

For a moment neither of them spoke.

Then Erin tilted her head slightly.

"So," she said, "your coworkers thought it would be funny to send a prostitute to your room."

Dan exhaled. "Apparently."

"And they expected… what exactly?"

He gave a helpless shrug.

"I'm a bit of a nerd. Straight-laced, I think you called it."

"That's depressing."

Dan laughed quietly.

"You should hear what passes for entertainment at social work conventions. Sometimes we make light of the same situations we spend all day dealing with. Dark humor."

Erin smiled slightly.

"I imagine the bar is low."

"It is."

Another voice echoed faintly down the hallway, followed by the ding of an elevator.

Erin took another sip of coffee.

"So you're really married?" she asked.

Dan nodded.

"Very."

She studied him.

"You didn't hesitate."

"About what?"

"Telling me to leave."

Dan shrugged.

"I like my life."

"That's rare."

"What is?"

"People who say that and actually mean it."

Dan tilted his head slightly.

"You don't believe in marriage?"

Erin considered the question.

"I believe in the idea of it."

"That sounds cautious."

"Observation," she said.

Dan leaned back in his chair.

"Observation from where?"

She gave a small smile.

"From watching people."

"That seems to be a theme with you."

"It's part of the job."

Dan nodded slowly. "I guess it would be."

She set the coffee cup down and looked at him again.

"So you never worry about temptation?"

Dan laughed softly.

"I'm sitting in a hotel room with a prostitute drinking coffee."

"Fair point."

"And yet," he added, "I'm still drinking coffee."

Erin smirked.

"You're very disciplined."

"No," he said. "I'm very happy."

She studied him carefully now.

"That sounds like something someone tells themselves."

Dan chuckled.

"Possibly."

"But I've been married twelve years," he said. "You learn a few things."

"Like what?"

"Like fidelity isn't really about temptation."

"What is it about?"

"Decision."

Erin leaned back slightly.

"That sounds philosophical."

"It's practical."

"How so?"

Dan shrugged.

"You don't wake up every morning feeling romantic."

"No?"

"No."

"That's disappointing."

"But you can wake up every morning deciding who you're going to be loyal to."

Erin thought about that.

The ice machine clattered again down the hall.

"You must be a good social worker," she said.

"Why?"

"You believe people can make better choices."

Dan smiled faintly.

"That's the whole job."

Erin picked up the coffee again, watching the steam rise from the cup. Dan's words settled uneasily in her thoughts.

Decision over temptation.

Loyalty as a choice.

She took a slow sip, the bitterness lingering on her tongue longer than the warmth.

"And if they don't?" she asked quietly.

"Then we try to help the kids who have to live with their choices," Dan said. "Whatever people decide, the children still have to grow up inside those decisions."

The room fell quiet again.

After a moment Dan reached into his jacket pocket and pulled out a small card.

He set it on the table between them.

"If you ever run into a situation like the one you were asking about," he said, "call me."

Erin glanced down.

The card read:

Daniel Harper

Child Protection Services

A phone number sat neatly beneath the title.

She didn't touch it at first.

For a moment she simply stared at it, the weight of her own circumstances pressing quietly against her chest. Trust was not something she gave easily. Too many promises, too many systems that claimed to help but rarely did.

She blinked quickly, forcing back the faint sting behind her eyes.

"Why would you do that?" she asked.

Dan shrugged.

"You asked the kind of questions people ask when they're worried about someone."

He paused.

"And sometimes people just need a place to start."

Erin looked at the card a moment longer.

Then she slid it across the table and tucked it into her purse.

"You might regret that," she said lightly.

Dan smiled.

"I doubt it."

Down the hallway the ice machine roared to life again.

Erin stood.

"Well," she said, smoothing the fabric of her dress, "your two hours are still running."

Dan checked his watch.

"We've got about ninety minutes left."

She smiled faintly.

"Then I suppose we should decide whether to keep talking… or let your coworkers think you got their money's worth."

Dan leaned back in his chair. "They're probably drunk by now. I doubt they even remember how long you've been here."

Erin paused at the door. Then she turned back toward him.

"I take it you don't drink either, Dan Harper?"

"I don't."

"Figures."

She gave a knowing half-smile.

"You know, my grandmother used to say there was no such thing as coincidence. Only meetings arranged by God."

She studied him.

"You strike me as someone who believes that."

"I do."

She tilted her head slightly.

"I don't."

"Why not?"

Erin rested her hand on the door handle. For a brief moment she thought of her grandmother; the quiet certainty in the old woman's voice whenever she spoke about faith.

Erin had never shared that certainty.

"Because coincidences," she said softly, "usually turn out to be problems waiting to reveal themselves."

Dan studied her for a moment.

"Or solutions."

She gave a small, unreadable smile.

"We'll see."

Chapter Four

…for the first time in a long while, Erin knows exactly where she's going. – Erin

The click of the hotel room door punctures the air behind her.

The corridor is a tunnel of low gold light and institutional carpet, the kind that swallows color into beige anonymity. Erin walks, one measured step after another, the echoes of her heels retreating toward the elevator's polished chrome mouth. The smell of stale coffee lingers in the air, mixed with the resinous grind of the ice machine digesting another load in its mechanical gut.

She walks slowly at first. Dan Harper still occupies the front of her mind; the careful posture of his hands, the way he spoke about loyalty as if it were a discipline rather than a feeling.

Strange how quickly a stranger's words can find the old, unhealed places.

Erin has always drawn confidences from people. Most never realized it, but she catalogued everything they said. Every judgment. Every careless truth that slipped out when they thought no one was paying attention.

Cynical.

But useful.

She presses the elevator button with a little more force than necessary and watches the red numbers descend.

Erin studies herself in the brass paneling beside the doors. The reflection is warped, stretched thin by the cheap metal. A woman in borrowed glamour stares back at her, the pale wig sitting on her skull like an afterthought.

She should take it off.

Not yet.

Not until she's outside.

A soft chime. The elevator opens.

She steps inside alone. The air smells faintly of cheap cologne. A long brown hair clings to the seam of the wall. Erin pinches it between two fingers and studies it for a moment, wondering whose life it once belonged to, before letting it fall.

The ride down is brief.

The doors open to the lobby. The night clerk glances up, recognizes her as someone passing through, and gives the brief nod of a man trained not to notice things.

He's young, with hands too long for his body, drumming lightly on the faux-granite counter. His eyes slide away from hers almost immediately. Whether from politeness or indifference, she can't tell.

Past the desk the lobby opens wide and quiet. Erin walks through it without slowing.

Her mind is still upstairs.

Still sitting across from Dan Harper.

Still hearing him talk about loyalty as if it were something people practiced the way others practiced prayer.

What was that, exactly?

Two hours that weren't supposed to exist.

She had knocked expecting the usual script; small talk, negotiation, performance. Instead she left with a social worker's business card tucked in her purse and a head full of questions she didn't want to examine too closely.

The glass doors slide open as she approaches.

Outside, the city breathes humid air against her face.

The parking lot glows under sodium lights. Somewhere a car alarm chirps halfheartedly before giving up.

Erin steps under the awning and reaches up, peeling the wig from her head with practiced ease. Cool air touches the damp roots of her real hair. For a moment she stands there, strangely exposed.

She turns once and looks back at the hotel.

Bright lights. Clean windows. A building that promises nothing and keeps that promise perfectly.

Her phone vibrates in her coat pocket.

She pulls it out.

The screen shows a message from Jamie.

Her brother.

He never texts this late.

Erin slips the phone back into her pocket and walks toward the sanctuary of her car.

Behind her, the hotel's glow fades with every step.

The phone's screen lights the car interior when she unlocks it.

Jamie's message waits on the screen.

"*u alive? how's school. did u see UNC lost again lol*"

On the surface it reads like the usual nonsense he sends her late at night.

But something about it sits wrong.

Jamie never texts like that.

She slides into the driver's seat and closes the door.

The parking lot is mostly empty now, just a battered minivan and a maintenance truck idling across the lot.

Erin could answer with something quick. Alive. Tired. Don't care about UNC.

Instead she presses call.

Jamie answers on the second ring.

"Hey."

His voice is soft, still caught halfway between boy and man.

"Hey yourself," Erin says. "You still up?"

"Yeah." Something clatters in the background. A spoon against a bowl maybe. "Thought you'd be out. It's Friday."

Erin studies her reflection in the dark windshield.

"Just got out of a thing," she says. "What's up?"

A pause.

"Not much. Dad's watching TV. Mom's… you know."

Erin exhales slowly.

"At the casino?"

"Yeah. She left after dinner."

"What did you eat?"

"Frozen pizza."

The answer comes too quickly.

Erin doesn't push it.

"You coming home this weekend?" Jamie asks.

"I can't. I've got work tomorrow."

"Oh."

She hears the small door close in his voice.

"How's school?" she asks.

"Fine."

A beat.

"We got progress reports," he adds. "I'm not failing anything."

Erin nods even though he can't see it.

"Good."

Silence stretches between them.

Then Jamie asks quietly, "You doing okay?"

The question catches her off guard.

"Yeah," she says. "Just tired."

"Don't stress," he says. "If you need help with math let me know. I'm basically a genius now."

She smiles despite herself.

"I believe it."

Something creaks in the background behind him.

Erin's voice lowers.

"Is Dad mad?"

Jamie answers too quickly.

"No. He's chill. Just tired."

She waits.

The silence grows heavier.

Finally he says, quieter now, "He was mad earlier. It's nothing."

"Did he hit you?"

"No," Jamie says.

A beat too late.

"Just yelled."

"About what?"

"The garage."

"Did you clean it?"

Jamie laughs once.

"It was already clean."

Erin closes her eyes.

"I'm sorry."

"Not your fault."

They sit there listening to the faint sound of a television somewhere in the background.

"Call me if it gets worse," she says softly.

Jamie doesn't answer.

But she knows he hears her.

"Night, Jamie."

"Night."

He hangs up first.

Erin stares at the phone for a long moment before lowering it.

In the passenger seat her purse sits open. Dan Harper's card peeks from the edge like something alive.

Jamie's voice fades, but the memory of him pulls Erin backward.

Back to the house on Ann Street.

Four years hasn't dulled the details.

The beige linoleum tiles curling at the corners. The smell of burnt coffee that never left the kitchen. Her father's voice filling the rooms like smoke.

One winter night Jamie had been sitting on the couch with a Rubik's cube, turning it slowly in his hands.

Her mother had found a small plastic bag in the car earlier that day and set it on the kitchen counter like evidence in a trial.

When their father walked in and saw it, his face turned red instantly.

"Is this yours?" he demanded.

Jamie looked up from the cube.

"What?"

"This." The bag snapped in the air. "Your pot."

"I've never—"

"Bullshit."

The shouting came fast after that.

Jamie's shoulders folded inward as if trying to shrink away from the sound.

From the kitchen doorway Erin watched it all unfold.

She should have said something.

Should have pointed out that Jamie hadn't even been in the car that weekend.

She should have said she'd seen their father smoking pot on the back porch some nights when he thought no one could see him.

Wanted to say the bag probably belonged to him.

Wanted to say the truth mattered.

But in that house truth rarely changed anything.

Her father grabbed Jamie by the collar and dragged him down the hallway.

The bedroom door slammed hard enough to shake the walls.

Later Erin knocked quietly on Jamie's door.

He was sitting on the edge of the bed, Rubik's cube still in his hands.

Half solved.

"Hey," she said.

"Hey."

"You okay?"

Jamie forced a small smile.

"It's fine," he said.

He turned the cube once more in his hands.

"Just tell Mom I'm not hungry."

Erin left him there.

The cube still half finished.

The Civic sits silent in the parking lot.

Condensation gathers along the inside of the windshield, turning the streetlights into blurred halos.

Erin checks her phone again.

No other messages from Jamie while she was in the hotel.

She leans back in the seat and stares through the fogged glass.

He has survived four years in that house since she left.

Four years of learning when to stay quiet.

Four years of pretending everything is fine.

They both knew the routine to keep the peace in the house.

She reaches into her purse and pulls out Dan Harper's card.

Daniel Harper

Child Protection Services

The card feels heavier than paper should.

She turns it over between her fingers.

Saving someone, she has learned, is rarely dramatic.

Mostly it's patience.

Waiting.

Collecting the small pieces until they finally add up to something you can use.

For now the card goes back into her wallet.

Not tonight.

Across the lot a man in a suit smokes a cigarette beside his car.

The battered minivan pulls away, its taillights painting the asphalt red before disappearing into the dark.

Her phone buzzes.

Jamie again.

A meme this time, some pixelated cat with laser eyes and the words *Monday mood.*

Erin exhales a small laugh.

She sends back a thumbs-up and a string of emojis.

The engine starts with a quiet shudder.

Streetlights hum overhead.

Erin grips the steering wheel.

"Just a little more time," she says quietly.

No one hears it but her.

The car rolls forward.

Behind her the hotel lights fade into the night.

Ahead, the road stretches empty and uncertain.

But for the first time in a long while, Erin knows exactly where she's going.

Chapter Five

Can we talk sometime? - Erin

Monday nights in the Harper house move in slow loops: the kettle's thin whistle, the low drone of the dishwasher, the weight of case files left open on the coffee table.

Dan Harper's living room, if it can be called that, is less a room than a corridor of triage, where social worker and husband blur together until it's hard to tell which one he's supposed to be. A pale blue Ikea rug curls at the corners. The sofa is the color of dried toothpaste. The ceiling light flickers whenever someone runs the microwave.

Dan sits cross-legged on the floor, reviewing the latest home assessment, when someone pounds on the door with the theatrical violence of old friends.

He checks his phone. Early.

Not by much.

He stands, running a hand through hair that has never cooperated with gravity. For a moment he glances down the hallway toward the kitchen.

Sarah isn't visible.

A small relief. She tolerates his coworkers.

Dan opens the door to a wall of takeout bags and three people exhaling the smells of coffee and exhaustion.

Ben steps inside first. He wears the same trench coat year-round and claims it's "for the optics."

"You look like shit," Ben says.

"Thank you," Dan replies. "I learned from the best."

Nadia follows, her ponytail pulled so tight it lifts her eyebrows. Her sarcasm is legendary at the office. Her binders are color-coded.

Behind her is Martin, six months out of grad school and already aware that everyone in Child Protective Services is, deep down, replaceable.

They pile in without ceremony. Shoes kicked aside, coats tossed over chairs.

Takeout containers land on the coffee table beside the case files. Their lids are labeled in Sharpie.

HOT

NO NUTS

BEN ONLY

Martin drops onto the rug and nudges aside a child's crayon drawing sticking out of a work folder.

"Sarah not here?"

"Kitchen," Dan says.

"Is she hiding from us," Nadia asks, examining the drawing, "or the children?"

"You know we don't have children," Dan says without looking up. "Just evidence of them."

They laugh.

Dan manages a small smile.

Drinks appear, wine for Nadia, microbrews for Ben and Martin, lukewarm green tea for Dan.

Conversation fills the room in stitches where silence might otherwise take hold: office rumors, budget cuts, intake procedures. From the kitchen, the sounds of Sarah moving, knife on cutting board, running water, punctuate the gaps.

It is Ben, predictably, who brings up the conference.

"So, Harper," he says, leaning forward with theatrical gravity. "How's it feel to be the only person here who's been offered a full-service escort by a top-notch agency?"

Dan freezes, mug halfway to his mouth.

Martin coughs beer onto the rug.

Nadia slaps his back.

Dan sets the mug down carefully.

"That's not—"

But they're already laughing.

Ben lowers his voice like he's sharing classified information.

"Nothing but the best for our golden boy. You realize they billed it as 'services,' right? Charged it to the grant."

Dan glances toward the kitchen.

Sarah is visible for a moment, scraping carrot peels into the compost bin.

Her shoulders pause.

She doesn't turn around.

Dan says, louder than necessary, "It was a prank. And it wasn't funny."

"Oh come on," Martin says, flushed with beer and safety in numbers. "You must have at least thought about it."

Nadia catches Dan's eye.

"Harper's the only man here with an intact marriage," she says. "Of course he didn't do anything."

Ben grins.

"You're married to the job, man. We figured you needed to remember you're still alive."

Martin lifts his bottle.

"Yeah. Just to let you know you're alive."

The laughter bounces around the room.

Dan forces a smile that doesn't last long.

His ears ring with the words escort and conference like a faint alarm.

"Can we talk about something else?"

They do.

Overcompensating, perhaps.

Nadia tells a story about a baby found alone in a motel room. Ben counters with a custody exchange that happened in a parking lot at midnight. Martin offers one about a mother who arrived to a court date carrying a ferret in her purse.

Dan laughs when expected. Adds a story about twins who lived in a car for three days.

The stories build and overlap the way they always do among people who share this work.

From the kitchen, Sarah remains a quiet gravitational force.

Sometimes he sees her reflection in the microwave door. Sometimes just her silhouette in the patio glass.

He wonders how much she heard.

He tries to be louder. Kinder. The version of himself he sometimes imagines through the lens of his work—someone useful. Someone who fixes things.

Eventually the food disappears.

Ben falls asleep on the couch.

Nadia texts her ex.

Martin rinses bottles in the sink.

Dan stands in the hallway rehearsing how he'll explain the evening once the house is empty.

Sarah appears there instead.

Her face half-shadowed by the hallway light. "Did you know they'd do that?" she asks.

Dan shakes his head quickly. "It was a joke. A bad one."

She nods.

But her mouth stays tight.

"I'm sorry," he says.

She studies him for a moment. As if weighing the man she sees against the one she has constructed over years, social worker, husband, witness to too much.

The math doesn't always come out clean.

Finally she says, "You work too much."

Dan laughs quietly.

He's about to respond.

But she's already turned away.

Her slippers whisper across the linoleum as she returns to the kitchen.

Dan checks the locks, he finds Ben's hand resting on a child's drawing from his work file, a bright crayon sun over a stick-figure family.

Dan gently lifts the page and smooths the crease.

The house settles into silence.

Only the fridge hums.

And the memory of voices slowly fading from the walls.

After Ben's joke and Sarah's quiet retreat, the evening resumes in a lower key.

Martin wipes gravy from his chin and asks Dan, "So what's your call on the Thompson house? Foster placement or relatives?"

Dan shrugs.

"No relatives clean enough to qualify. There's a grandmother three states away but she's never met the kid. Probably temporary foster. Maybe a month."

Ben takes a drink.

"You ever get used to that?"

Nadia pours more wine.

"No one gets used to it," she says. "That's the point. The day you do, you're a monster."

Martin laughs.

"Or you quit. Like half my cohort already did."

Dan leans back against the couch.

"You learn to metabolize it," he says. "Or pretend you do. Some days you just carry it home and let it rot in your gut."

Nadia raises her glass.

"To the rot."

"To the rot," Ben echoes.

Martin hesitates before clinking his bottle. "And to the kids who don't end up case numbers."

The room quiets.

Stories begin to surface, cases that stick.

Nadia tells one about a girl who refused to speak for months.

Ben remembers a boy who practiced tying shoelace knots in his shelter bed.

Martin describes holding a baby for two hours during an intake while the mother was being arrested.

Dan finally says, "There were siblings once. Seven and four. Parents both opioid. The girl would only eat canned food if the label was still on. Said it was 'safer that way.'"

He pauses.

"Her brother chewed the metal lid open once and cut his mouth. Needed stitches."

Martin looks down at his bottle.

"I hope they're okay."

"They're together," Dan says.

"Some days that's the best you get."

The clock creeps toward ten.

Chairs scrape. Dishes stack.

Ben pulls on his trench coat.

"Same time next month?"

"Unless one of us quits," Nadia says.

"Or gets promoted," Dan adds.

They all groan.

At the door Ben claps Dan on the shoulder.

"Take it easy, Harper. And tell Sarah thanks."

"I will."

Headlights sweep the driveway as they pull away.

Dan stands in the doorway a moment longer than necessary.

Then he closes the door quietly.

Inside, the living room looks hollowed out; bottles, napkins, empty cartons.

He gathers the mess slowly.

The echo of laughter fades faster than the echo of need.

When the room is clean again he sits on the couch, rubbing his eyes.

For a moment the quiet almost feels like peace.

Almost.

Later the house settles into the silence that follows company.

Dan moves through the rooms checking lights and locks.

In the kitchen Sarah wipes a counter that's already clean.

Their movements orbit each other the way long marriages do.

Their fingers brush briefly over a drying glass.

"I'm going to shower," she says. "Don't stay up too late."

He nods.

After she leaves the room the quiet deepens.

Dan opens his laptop but doesn't read anything.

His phone vibrates.

The screen lights the table.

MISTY: *Can we talk sometime?*

He stares at the name.

Misty.

Ridiculous. Stagey.

But it's the only name he has.

Water runs in the bathroom down the hall.

When Sarah returns, hair damp, she notices the phone immediately.

Dan turns the screen toward her.

"It's her," he says. "The woman from the hotel."

Sarah waits.

"She didn't… do what they hired her for," he says. "We talked instead. About families. About the system. She seemed worried about a kid."

Sarah studies him.

"Okay," she says. "That's what I figured."

He talks more than he should.

"I saved her number in case she needed help. Social services, referrals… anything."

Sarah nods again.

But something hangs in the air between them.

They eat leftovers in silence.

She talks about a customer at the bookstore.

He tells her about a new case.

But every few minutes her eyes drift back to the phone.

Later, when Dan goes to brush his teeth, Sarah remains in the kitchen.

The phone lies on the table.

Dark now.

She considers picking it up.

Her hand stops halfway.

In the quiet the phone lights again.

MISTY: *Or not. I understand.*

Sarah watches the message fade.

She doesn't wake Dan.

She doesn't respond.

She just stands there a long time, the weight of two messages settling into the quiet spaces of the house.

Not accusation.

Not yet.

But not trust either.

Chapter Six

Thank you for trying. - Erin

Erin balances the phone on her thigh, its blue light washing over a law textbook. The word *estoppel* is underlined three times in red ink.

On the table sits a white business card.

Daniel Harper, LCSW

Child Protection Services

She has memorized the number.

The couch springs sag beneath her weight. The apartment smells faintly of dust and instant noodles. Legal pads cover the table, arguments scribbled, crossed out, rewritten. A small stack of unopened bills leans against a plastic novelty toy someone left here months ago as a joke she never bothered to remove.

She opens a text.

"Hey, not sure if you remember me but—"

Delete.

Another.

"Dear Mr. Harper, I require your professional advice—"

Delete.

The third is shorter.

"Is it safe to file an anonymous report?"

She stares at it. Too obvious.

Delete.

Erin picks up the card and runs her thumb along the raised letters of Harper's name.

Then she types again.

Sorry to text after hours the other day. Just wondering. What are the steps if someone suspects a child is living in a dangerous home?

Her finger hovers.

She presses **send.**

The phone buzzes almost immediately.

Dan Harper: *No worries. Anyone can call CPS with a concern and stay anonymous. We check every credible report. Is there a specific situation?*

Erin exhales slowly.

Just a general question, she types. *A friend growing up had parents who fought a lot. I always wondered when something crosses the line.*

She hesitates, then adds:

Not about me.

The reply takes longer this time.

Dan Harper: *There's not really a hard line. If a kid's safety might be at risk, it's worth reporting. Domestic violence, substance abuse, neglect, those are all reasons we check in. Did something happen recently?*

Erin leans back and studies the ceiling. Old water stains spread across the plaster like maps. Through the wall, a neighbor's television laughs at something.

She types again.

If someone drinks a lot, but only at night, yells constantly and the kid still goes to school… is that enough for a visit?

Three dots appear.

Disappear.

Return.

Dan Harper: *We get calls for less than that. If alcohol affects the home or the child seems afraid, we'd check on it.*

Her grip tightens on the phone.

She thinks of Jamie standing barefoot in the January snow, convinced the dog would freeze if he didn't rescue it from the garage.

What if the parent knows how to act normal for social workers? she writes. *Like they're fine when someone's watching.*

This reply comes slowly.

Dan Harper: *That happens more than you'd think. Kids usually find ways to signal something's wrong, even if it's subtle.*

Erin presses the phone against her thigh until the shaking in her hands fades.

She tries to end the conversation.

Thanks for the info. Just curious.

But another message appears.

Dan Harper: *If you want, I can walk you through the reporting process. You don't have to figure it out alone.*

The screen dims in her reflection.

One more message appears.

Dan Harper: *I'm here if you need anything else, Misty.*

The name catches her off guard.

She sets the phone down and wraps her arms around her knees.

She doesn't answer.

Not that night.

Tuesday mornings in the office are loud.

Phones ringing. The printer coughing out paperwork older than most of the interns. Someone reheating leftovers that smell like burnt garlic.

Dan works with the lights off, the glow of his monitor filling the room.

A new intake report waits in the queue.

Anonymous concern. Possible emotional abuse. Possible alcohol use in home.

He reads the report once.

Then again.

Something about the wording feels familiar.

Even if the parent is clever… even if it only happens when no one else is watching.

He flags the case for follow-up.

The process is routine now; background search, prior calls, school attendance records. Muscle memory. He schedules a visit on his calendar.

The address sits in the older part of town. Small brick houses. Chain-link fences. Lawns that gave up years ago.

He parks across the street and waits a moment.

The blinds twitch.

Then go still.

Dan walks up the porch steps and knocks.

The mother answers wearing a robe and a look that says she already hates him.

"Can I help you?"

Dan flashes his badge. "Just doing a routine welfare check."

She snorts. "He hasn't missed a day of school."

"Mind if I come in?"

A long pause.

Then she steps aside.

The house smells faintly of cigarettes and something fried hours ago. Not filthy. Just tired.

A man appears in the hallway.

"Who's this?"

"CPS," the woman says.

The boy stands behind him.

Jamie.

Thin. Watchful.

Dan offers a small wave.

"Mind if we talk outside for a minute?"

The father doesn't like that. The mother shrugs. Dan follows the kid as the parents seem not to care a stranger from the government is in the home.

They sit on the back steps.

Dead grass. Rusted buckets.

"How's school?" Dan asks.

"Fine."

"Things okay at home?"

Jamie shrugs.

Dan tries again.

"Sometimes when there's a lot of yelling, it makes things rough for kids."

Jamie stares at the fence.

"Not really."

Silence stretches between them.

Dan finally asks, "Anything you want to talk about?"

Jamie shakes his head.

"No offense," he says quietly, "but I've had enough therapy for a lifetime."

Dan nods.

He knows when to stop pushing.

As he leaves through the kitchen, Dan's eyes moved automatically across the room; sink, counter, refrigerator. The refrigerator handle had a small brass padlock through it.

He paused half a second too long.

The mother followed his gaze.

"Kid eats everything in the house," she said with a laugh. "We had to do something."

Dan nodded like it was normal.

But it wasn't.

Waiting becomes its own routine.

Erin checks her phone too often. Pretends she isn't.

Days pass.

Jamie still goes to school.

No updates.

No calls.

On Friday night, a message appears.

Dan Harper: *Followed up on the case. Family was defensive but nothing actionable. Kid says everything's fine. I'll keep an eye out, but unless someone comes forward there isn't much we can do.*

Erin reads it twice.

A weight settles in her chest.

Thank you for trying, she types.

After a moment:

Dan Harper: *Sometimes these things take time. The process is slow. But it isn't blind.*

Erin stares at the screen.

You do good work, she replies.

The message shows as read.

But nothing else comes.

That night she dreams of Jamie standing in the snow again, arms wrapped around himself, calm in a way that feels wrong.

When she wakes before dawn, the decision is already there.

She'll find a way through the system.

Somehow.

Chapter Seven

Kids lie sometimes...To protect the people they're afraid of. - *Erin*

Morning at Child Protection Services begins before the coffee finishes brewing.

Phones ring across the bullpen. Printers grind through paperwork. Someone argues softly over a case number while another worker laughs too loudly at something that isn't very funny.

Dan Harper stands with a mug in his hand and watches the room wake up. The office looks assembled from leftover furniture and modest expectations; half walls, mismatched chairs, motivational posters laminated sometime during the Clinton administration.

Through the smudged window behind his desk, a strip-mall parking lot fills slowly with delivery trucks. He sets the coffee down and surveys the stack of files waiting for him.

New intakes. Active investigations. A few cases that have been open long enough the folders look tired.

He sits and opens the first file.

Halfway through a progress note: *Client states she no longer has thoughts of self-harm but asked if her child could be adopted by a celebrity*, a head appears over the cubicle wall.

Mallory.

She still wears blazers that look recently purchased and slightly too formal for the office.

"Harper, you got a second?"

Dan gestures her in.

"Shoot."

She sits and slides a file across his desk.

"Beaudoin case. Supervisor's out and intake wants it signed off before noon."

Dan reads quickly. Drug abuse. Truancy. The familiar rhythm of generational damage written in careful language.

"You marked reunification as probable," he says.

Mallory nods.

"Mother's clean two months. Treatment confirms it. Kid's back in school every day."

Dan taps the page with his pen.

"Did you ask the kid where she wants to live?"

Mallory hesitates.

"She said home… but she also told the visitation monitor she likes foster care. I figured she was just being polite."

Dan slides the folder back.

"Never assume politeness means safety. Schedule another visit. Talk to her alone."

Mallory nods quickly.

"Thanks, Dan."

She leaves.

At 9:30 an alert pops up across the office monitors.

EMERGENCY PLACEMENT – NEED TRANSPORT

Dan pushes his chair back before the message finishes loading.

In the bullpen Nadia is already gathering volunteers.

"Six-year-old found at a school traffic stop," she says. "No guardian. Pajamas and rain boots. Father's record is a carnival ride."

Dan raises a hand.

"I'll drive."

Nadia nods.

"Of course you will."

The girl sits in the school conference room hugging a stuffed bear with matted fur and one mismatched button eye.

Dan kneels to her level.

"Is this yours?"

She grabs it instantly.

"His name is Cheese."

Dan nods.

"Cheese is a good name."

She studies him with the suspicion of someone who has already learned that adults change.

"I'm Dan," he says. "I'm here to make sure you're safe."

She says nothing.

On the ride back she presses her face into the bear and watches the passing buildings through the car window.

The foster parent arrives an hour later; prepared, calm, blankets already waiting.

The girl leaves without crying.

She does not wave goodbye.

By the time Dan sits back at his desk it is 2:22 PM.

His sandwich has hardened into something structural.

A sticky note is crooked on his monitor.

LOCKED FRIDGE

The memory returns instantly.

Jamie's kitchen.

The refrigerator secured with a small padlock.

Jamie had shrugged.

"Dad says it's so I don't eat all the food."

Dan remembers the father laughing from the living room. The sound hadn't been friendly.

He opens an email to Nadia.

Subject: Jamie Carter

No evidence last visit but something felt off. Requesting another check-in after hours. I can take it.

He pauses, then adds one line.

Also noticed a lock on the refrigerator. Probably nothing but worth noting.

He sends the email and leans back.

The phones keep ringing.

They always do.

By the time Dan pulls into the garage dusk has settled over the neighborhood.

Inside, the kitchen light is on.

Sarah stands at the stove stirring something that smells like onions and garlic.

"You're late," she says without turning.

"Emergency placement."

She chops celery.

"Did you eat lunch?"

"Not really."

"You're going to make yourself sick again."

Dan tries a smile.

"Smells good. Lentil soup?"

She doesn't answer but ladles it into bowls.

They sit.

He tells her about the six-year-old.

"How she held onto the stuffed bear the whole drive," he says. "Wouldn't let go."

Sarah listens quietly.

Then she asks, "Do you remember tomorrow?"

Dan's stomach sinks.

Her father's birthday dinner.

"Yes," he says quickly. "I'll be there."

"Don't bring your laptop."

"I won't."

Sarah studies him.

"Sometimes it feels like your real family is at that office."

Dan doesn't argue.

After a moment she asks,

"Why do you keep doing it?"

He thinks about the girl and the stuffed bear.

"Because it matters."

Sarah's expression softens slightly.

"You can't save everyone, Dan."

"I know."

She looks at him for a long moment.

"Do you even know when you're home anymore?"

Neither of them answers.

They finish dinner quietly.

Later that night Dan sits in the small office at the back of the house.

Paperwork first.

Emails.

Case notes.

Routine keeps the day from following him into sleep.

But eventually his phone lights up when it is finished charging.

The message thread labeled **Misty** is on top of the message list.

He rereads the conversation.

The messages are careful.

Every sentence measured.

He scrolls upward and notices something he missed before.

The timestamps.

12:47 AM.

1:12 AM.

2:03 AM.

Every message came after midnight.

Dan leans back.

Most people who contacted CPS called during the day.

Teachers.

Neighbors.

Relatives.

Whoever Misty was, she only asked questions when the rest of the world had gone quiet.

He rereads one line.

Is there a threshold?

That word catches him again.

Most callers didn't talk like that.

They said things like *when is it bad enough* or *should I be worried.*

Threshold sounded almost clinical.

Then there was the first question she asked.

About anonymous reporting.

Most people didn't know that was an option until he explained it.

Dan studies the screen.

Whoever she was, she had thought about this before reaching out.

He opens her number.

Local.

He could call.

But protocol says you let informants come forward when they're ready.

He sets the phone down.

Still, something about the conversation doesn't sit right.

Intelligent.

Articulate.

Not what he expected from someone working the street.

Then again, he realizes, he doesn't actually know what to expect.

He turns off the lamp.

But sleep takes a while.

Dawn pushes through the blinds in thin gray lines.

Dan stands on the front step with a mug of coffee while the street wakes slowly.

Delivery trucks.

Newspapers hitting pavement.

The ordinary machinery of morning.

He thinks about the kids he has helped.

The ones who ended up safe. The ones who didn't.

Jamie's face drifts into the space between those thoughts.

The way the boy sat on the back step.

Answering every question carefully.

Watching the window behind Dan's shoulder before he spoke. Dan wonders again what he missed.

His phone vibrates with any texts received during the night while he was asleep.

Misty's number.

A text message.

Did you ever wonder if the kid was telling the truth?

Dan frowns.

Another message appears.

Kids lie sometimes. Not to cause trouble.

To protect the people they're afraid of.

The words settle heavily in his chest.

He watches the screen.

Sorry to bother you so late. Just hoping you eventually meet the threshold for intervention.

Dan notices the phrasing. The late time of night that she texted. All odd.

Dan pockets the phone and heads to the car.

He has a feeling the day is about to get complicated.

And he still doesn't know who Misty really is.

Chapter Eight

How did you get here? - Erin

She presses the iron to the robe as if the act might cauterize the years. Steam hisses from the plate. The sound reminds her of train brakes, of doors closing, of time collapsing into small decisive moments. Subsidized apartments. Quiet kitchens. Temporary beds in rooms that were never hers.

Erin holds the fabric steady and guides the iron slowly across the polyester.

She has always been meticulous.

The robe absorbs the light instead of reflecting it, the black surface catching faint oily streaks where the steam passes. The sleeves hang absurdly long, ceremonial and oversized, as if every graduate is meant to look like a child playing dress-up.

She studies it. The robe looks studious, respectable. Nothing like the clothes that paid for it. She lifts the iron and rests it on its heel.

The apartment is barely seven hundred square feet and already packed to capacity. Casebooks stacked in precarious towers. Outlines spread across the futon. Post-it notes blooming from every surface like yellow petals.

The air smells faintly of starch and the ghost of a cheap vanilla candle burned to its wick. On the counter sits a loaf of bread in a plastic sleeve. Three eggs. A mug of water slowly cooling.

A few empty boxes lean against the wall.

Soon she will move somewhere better. At least that's the plan.

She glances at her phone.

Nothing.

No messages. No missed calls.

For a moment she is eight years old again and the phone is a god, its silence a verdict.

She tells herself she does not expect anything.

Her parents had scoffed when she mentioned graduation. Her mother laughed and said Erin always thought she was smarter than everyone else. Her father barely spoke when she stopped by the house last week to check on Jamie.

She had gone for Jamie.

Not them.

She lays the robe carefully across the sofa so it will not crease.

It had been the same for high school.

The same for college.

No parents.

Just her.

During high school graduation she had seen her father's truck drive past the football field where the ceremony was held. For a moment she thought he might be stopping.

Instead he kept driving toward the liquor store across town. To them, it had just been another day.

On the table sits the diploma envelope, sealed with the university's gold crest.

She considers opening it.

Just to prove it is real.

Instead she drapes her honor cords across the back of the only dining chair, red for pro bono work, blue for moot court, silver for undergraduate GPA.

They hang there like vestments.

She clips her hair back and smooths the loose strands in the mirror.

What the camera will see later is not joy exactly.

More like defiance.

The skin beneath her eyes is bruised purple from too little sleep.

She presses her thumbs against her eyelids, counting slowly to five, then lifts her chin and adjusts the clip so her jawline sharpens in the reflection.

It looks almost beautiful.

She decides to accept that.

At the table she cracks an egg into a chipped bowl. The yolk splits immediately, yellow bleeding into white. She beats it with a fork and cooks it quickly in a pan.

She eats standing up.

Efficient. Quiet.

When she finishes she rinses the bowl, dries it, sets it upside down on the rack.

Routine is the only thing she trusts.

The phone again.

Still nothing.

She packs her bag.

Phone. Keys. Wallet. Lint roller. A Ziploc with safety pins.

She pauses once more at the door.

For a second she lets herself feel it. All the nights she worked while the rest of the city slept. The men who called her Misty. The professors who called her Miss Carter. Jamie's voice on the phone late at night, whispering updates about home.

All of them are here with her now.

Witnesses.

She opens the door and steps into the hallway. The corridor is cool and quiet. The robe swings from her arm as she walks toward the stairwell.

When the door closes behind her the echo sounds almost ceremonial.

A benediction.

Or a challenge.

Morning traffic moves in slow bursts along the curb. Jamie stands outside a small plexiglass bus shelter, hands shoved into the pockets of a borrowed shirt. The collar rubs against his neck. He keeps tugging at it as if loosening a rope.

A folded scrap of paper sits in his pocket.

Two bus routes.

One transfer.

Erin's handwriting.

He checks it again.

A car door shuts nearby.

Jamie looks up.

Dan Harper steps onto the sidewalk with a messenger bag slung across his shoulder. Without his tie he looks almost casual, but the way he scans the street is the same, quietly alert.

Jamie lowers his head.

Too late.

Dan recognizes him immediately.

"Jamie?"

Jamie stiffens.

Dan walks closer, puzzled.

"What are you doing out here? Shouldn't you be at school?"

Jamie shrugs. "Had somewhere to go."

Dan studies him.

Different clothes. Clean shirt. Nervous energy.

"Your parents know where you are?" Dan asks.

Jamie nods quickly. "Yeah."

The lie hangs in the air.

Dan watches him another moment, then sighs. "Well," he says, "don't disappear on me."

Jamie glances up.

"What?"

"If you're going somewhere," Dan says, "make sure you come back."

Jamie nods.

Dan adjusts his bag and heads toward the campus lot.

Jamie waits until he disappears around the corner.

Only then does he breathe again.

The bus pulls up with a hydraulic sigh.

Jamie climbs aboard.

The auditorium smells like nylon and perfume.

Rows of black robes stretch in every direction. The air buzzes with cheap celebration and amplified speeches.

Erin finds her assigned seat and sits with the diploma envelope pressed beneath her palms.

The dean begins speaking.

Potential. Responsibility. Bright future.

The same recycled phrases every class hears.

Around her graduates shift in their chairs. Phones glow in hidden hands. Someone behind her whispers a running commentary.

Erin keeps her eyes forward.

She is not the next generation of anything.

She is simply herself.

That will have to be enough.

When her name is called—

"Erin Rose Carter."

—the sound of it echoes briefly across the hall.

She walks across the stage.

Handshake.

Diploma.

Flash of the photographer's camera.

Six seconds.

Three years of law school reduced to six seconds.

When she looks toward the audience the lights wash the faces into indistinct shapes.

Families wave.

Parents cheer.

Erin sees none of hers.

She reminds herself again she did not do this for them.

And then it is over.

Outside the sunlight hits like an explosion.

Families cluster everywhere; flowers, balloons, cameras. The noise is relentless.

Erin moves through the crowd slowly.

Near the edge of the quad she catches a glimpse of someone familiar.

Dan Harper.

Standing near the walkway.

Watching the crowd then shaking the hand of a graduate.

Her stomach tightens.

Without thinking she shifts direction slightly, turning away from him.

Then she sees Jamie.

He stands beneath an oak tree, shoulders tight, holding a wrinkled graduation program in both hands.

The paper has been folded and unfolded so many times the edges have gone soft.

For a moment she just stares.

"Jamie?" she calls.

He looks up immediately. His mouth twists into an uncertain smile.

When she reaches him, she says the only thing that comes out.

"How did you get here?"

"Bus," he says. "Transferred at the mall."

He glances at her robe. "You look… official."

She laughs softly. "I feel like a knockoff judge."

Jamie lifts the program slightly. "I saw you up there."

"You didn't smile," he adds.

"Not really my thing."

"Me neither."

He hesitates, then says quietly: "I didn't know if anyone else would come."

The words land harder than anything else he could have said. Erin pulls him into a hug before she can stop herself.

Jamie buries his face against the sleeve of her robe.

They stand there for several seconds while families celebrate all around them.

When she finally pulls away her face is wet.

"You know," she says softly, "you're the only one I wanted here."

Jamie shakes his head.

"You don't mean that."

She laughs through the tears.

"I do."

They walk away from the crowd and sit on the campus steps overlooking the lawn.

Jamie hugs his knees.

Erin rests the diploma across her lap.

After a while Jamie speaks.

"Now that you're a lawyer…"

He takes a breath.

"…can you get me out of there?"

The question hangs between them.

Erin studies his face.

The shadows beneath his eyes. The nervous way he picks at the scab on his wrist. The way he apologetically defends his every action. Softly. Humbly waiting on reaction.

"I can't take you today," she says carefully. "But I can make a plan."

Jamie nods slowly.

"I thought maybe it would be easier now."

Erin looks at the diploma.

"All this means," she says quietly, "is that now I know how to fight."

That earns a small smile.

Jamie checks his watch.

"Bus comes soon. If I catch this one they won't even know I slipped out."

She hugs him again before he leaves.

"Text me when you get home."

"I will."

She watches him walk away until he disappears around the corner. Then she opens her phone and begins searching.

Emancipation statutes.

Local shelters.

Family court precedents.

Names of sympathetic judges.

Victory, she realizes, is not applause.

Victory is building a ladder rung by rung until both of them can climb out.

She sits there in the sun until it begins to hurt.

Then she stands and starts walking home.

The future feels slightly less impossible than it did that morning.

Chapter Nine

When are we going to do it? - Erin

The last of the suds slip from the sponge as Sarah's fingers drags a bowl through the shallow sink water. The kitchen is an archetype of itself: towels folded, counters wiped dull with disinfectant, the radio murmuring beneath the steady rhythm of household news.

Outside, the yard glistens from late rain.

Upstairs, the pipes sing; Dan's shower, the deliberate cadence of someone finishing a long day.

It is nine-thirty. A nothing hour. In this house the hour has always belonged to routine: finish the kitchen, lock the doors, wipe the faucet dry.

Sarah checks the refrigerator for tomorrow's lunch, straightens a magnet on the freezer door, and only then notices the phone on the counter.

Not hers.

Dan's.

The screen pulses softly with a new message.

She pauses, hands still damp.

They are not a couple with secrets. Or at least they never needed to be. The years have flattened them into familiar patterns, predictable, safe.

The phone buzzes again.

The screen lights up.

Misty

Sarah cannot help but read the preview.

He didn't get hit tonight.

A second message follows.

You said to keep notes.

She freezes.

The name lands heavily in her mind, Misty. The escort. The joke from the conference months ago. The story Dan had told with that awkward half-smile, insisting nothing happened.

The phone vibrates again.

This time she picks it up.

The messages stretch back weeks.

At first they are clipped and professional.

This is Dan. You called about the Carter case?

Yes. Just wanted to know if it's safe to talk.

It's always safe.

Then the tone changes.

Bruise on his arm again.

School called about attendance.

He finally ate tonight. Mac and cheese.

When are we going to do it?

Sarah scrolls slowly.

You were right about anonymous reporting.

If the parents ask questions I'll say nothing.

And then tonight's message again.

He didn't get hit tonight.

Sarah reads it twice.

The words sit heavily in her stomach.

Maybe it is a case. Maybe Dan is helping someone. That is what he does.

But he never mentioned any of this.

Not the messages. Not the woman sending them.

Upstairs the shower shuts off.

Sarah places the phone exactly where it was. Face down. Perfectly aligned.

Dan comes downstairs moments later, hair damp, pajamas slightly twisted from sleepwear laziness.

He smiles at her, opens the refrigerator, grabs a seltzer.

Routine.

Sarah watches him carefully now.

He stands at the counter drinking, glancing casually around the kitchen.

The phone sits between them like something fragile.

She says finally, "How was work?"

Dan shrugs.

"Long. Too much paperwork."

She nods.

The radio hums quietly behind them.

For a moment she expects him to reach for the phone, to check it, maybe even explain.

But he doesn't.

He simply sets the can down and heads toward the stairs.

"You okay?" he asks casually.

Sarah smiles.

"Just tired."

He accepts that easily.

When he disappears upstairs, Sarah remains at the sink, the silence in the kitchen suddenly heavier than it should be.

Something has shifted.

And she knows it.

The bedroom is dim, cooled by the hesitant hum of the air conditioner. Sarah lies facing the wall, awake long before Dan comes to bed.

She hears everything; the phone placed on the nightstand, the rustle of sheets, the slow settling of his body beside hers.

Minutes pass.

Then she says quietly: "Who is Misty?"

The stillness in the room becomes immediate.

Dan turns toward her.

"What?"

"I saw the messages."

Her voice is steady. "I wasn't trying to pry. They just kept coming."

Dan exhales slowly.

"She's not what you think."

Sarah almost laughs.

"You mean not the prostitute your coworkers sent to your hotel room?"

The word hangs unpleasantly in the air.

Dan shakes his head.

"That was a prank. Nothing happened."

"Then why are you still talking to her?"

Dan sits up.

"She's connected to a case."

Sarah folds her arms. "And you can't tell me about it."

His expression tightens. "I legally can't."

Silence stretches between them.

Sarah studies his face carefully. "Are you sleeping with her?"

Dan recoils.

"No. Never."

She believes him.

That almost makes it worse.

"Then why hide it?" she asks quietly.

Dan stares at his hands.

"Because if the wrong people hear about it, someone could get hurt."

She hears the words but not the meaning.

All she hears is secrecy.

Sarah pulls the blanket around herself and stands.

"I'm tired."

She takes a pillow and leaves for the couch.

Dan sits alone in the dark bedroom long after she goes.

Weeks pass in small absences.

Sarah sleeps on the couch most nights.

Some mornings she wakes in the bed again, unsure when she moved back.

The house becomes quiet in new ways.

One night she wakes at 2:47 a.m.

Dan is asleep beside her.

The phone on the nightstand lights up.

Misty

Sarah does not reach for it. She simply watches the light fade.

Beside her Dan turns slightly in his sleep.

Sarah rolls away from him.

The distance between them now feels deliberate.

Silence becomes their routine.

Sarah leaves earlier for work. Dan stays later at the office.

Dinner becomes a quiet exchange of plates and short sentences.

Some nights they sit in the same room without speaking.

The phone glows occasionally on the counter.

Each time the same name appears.

Misty

The messages are clinical.

Bruise on ribs.

He skipped school again.

No incident tonight.

There is nothing romantic in them.

But Sarah sees only the name. The long hours at work.

And the secrecy.

One night Sarah sits alone at the kitchen table.

Dan is upstairs in the shower. A usual routine.

The house is quiet except for the refrigerator motor humming. Dan's phone vibrates again on the counter.

The screen lights.

Misty

Sarah doesn't read the message.

She no longer needs to.

Instead she opens her laptop.

Searches:

divorce lawyer near me

The results appear instantly. She reads none of them. She simply fills out the first consultation form.

Name.

Marriage date.

Reason for filing.

She hesitates.

Then types:

Infidelity, emotional distance

It is not exactly true.

But it is close enough for the story the world will believe. Dan's work has consumed him. It has consumed their marriage.

She submits the form.

The phone vibrates again behind her.

Sarah closes the laptop.

The decision is already made.

Dan comes home late the following evening.

Sarah is waiting in the living room. She hands him an envelope.

He opens it slowly.

Petition for Dissolution of Marriage

Dan reads the first page and stops.

"I'm sorry," he says quietly.

Sarah watches him.

"I can't live like this," she says. "The secrets. The way you disappear into your work."

Dan almost laughs.

"You'd think I worked for the CIA."

She doesn't smile.

"You trust a stranger more than your own wife."

Dan wants to explain.

He wants to tell her everything.

But doing that would destroy the case.

And possibly the boy.

So he says nothing.

Sarah stands.

"You used to be the most honest person I knew."

She walks upstairs.

Dan remains in the living room holding the papers.

His phone vibrates in his pocket.

A message from Misty.

He opens it.

I'm ready to move on the evidence we have.

Dan closes his eyes.

For a long time he does not move.

Chapter Ten

She wonders if her career is ending before it even began. - Erin

The morning arrives in flat increments of gray as Erin walks the final block to the firm in a suit that still smells faintly of thrift-store lemon cleaner. The building rises from the street like a sheet of glass folded into geometry. The kind of place she once associated with hedge funds and cosmetic dentistry.

Now she works here.

The lobby doors open without resistance. Inside, the space is quiet and polished; concrete floors, brushed steel, light filtered to remove any trace of the outside world. Erin crosses the vestibule slowly, aware of every step.

She is thirty minutes early.

Earlier than necessary, earlier than reasonable. As if arriving first might allow her to become part of the building before anyone decides she doesn't belong.

The elevator mirrors her from every angle. The suit fits almost perfectly. The collar refuses to lie flat.

She watches herself multiply in the glass.

Fourth floor.

The hallway smells like new carpet and expensive restraint. Matte black walls, oversized photographs of canyons, furniture arranged with surgical symmetry.

At the reception desk a placard reads:

Stein, Radcliffe & Dunn

Erin checks her phone.

Twenty-seven minutes early.

When the receptionist appears, she moves like someone already accustomed to being observed.

"You must be Ms. Carter."

"Erin. Yes. First day."

"Mr. Radcliffe will see you before the staff meeting."

They walk down the hall together. Erin's heels make a delicate clicking sound against the floor.

Radcliffe's office door stands open.

Inside, the room is stripped of personality. Glass desk. Dark wood. Three diplomas. One framed newspaper headline about a custody victory.

Radcliffe rises when she enters.

"You come highly recommended," he says, shaking her hand. "Your clinic work was impressive. I'm told when you interned here during law school you stood out."

"Thank you."

He gestures for her to sit.

"As you know, this is a family law practice," he continues. "Divorce, custody, domestic issues. The law matters, of course. But what really matters is narrative."

He leans back slightly.

"In the end, people just want the court to believe their story."

The words settle in Erin's chest like something she already knows.

"Most divorces aren't about law," Radcliffe adds. "They're about competing versions of reality."

She nods.

"Good," he says, standing. "You'll have a file waiting after the meeting. The best way to start is to jump in."

The conference room fills quickly. Associates slide into chairs with quiet confidence. The meeting is brisk; announcements, schedules, small victories from the week before.

By 9:18 it is over.

Erin finds her name on a temporary placard outside the last office.

Erin Carter – Associate

Inside, the office is just large enough for a desk and two chairs. A window looks out to the hallway rather than the city.

She places her phone carefully on the desk. Pens aligned. Legal pad centered.

From her bag she removes the only personal object she brought: a rubber dinosaur with its tail bitten off.

Jamie's.

She sets it behind the monitor.

Radcliffe's words linger in her mind.

People want the court to believe their story.

For the first time that morning, her nerves begin to settle.

At 10:00 a notification appears on her screen.

See me — Radcliffe

He slides a folder across the desk when she enters. "First assignment," he says.

Erin places her hand on the folder.

"Divorce case. Medium complexity, high conflict. Client claims her husband hired a prostitute at a conference and continued contacting her afterward."

The word lands harder than it should.

Radcliffe shrugs.

"There's a paper trail. Texts. Calls. Possibly a hotel receipt. If it checks out, it's a clean narrative. An easy case to get your feet wet."

A beat.

"Cheating with a prostitute is a bad look."

Erin keeps her face neutral.

"Do I meet the client alone?"

"Yes. Eleven o'clock."

She opens the folder slightly.

Client: Sarah Harper

Radcliffe adds one last thought before she leaves.

"Remember; clients don't want lawyers. They want someone to witness their pain."

In the hallway Erin exhales slowly.

Back in her office she opens the folder fully.

Sarah Harper.

The intake reads like most of them do; dates, places, a sequence of events.

Her husband returned from a conference claiming coworkers had sent a prostitute to his room as a joke. Later Sarah discovered months of messages between him and the same woman.

Erin flips to the call log.

The contact name written in the margin:

Misty

Her pulse jumps.

She tells herself it means nothing.

There are many men named Harper.

Many prostitutes who use that name.

She keeps reading.

Erin spreads the documents across the desk in careful rows.

Intake statement.

Timeline.

Message logs.

The texts appear ordinary at first glance.

Short exchanges.

Flat language.

Nothing romantic.

Nothing explicit.

Then a phrase catches her.

Here if you need to talk.

Another line.

Thank you. I'll keep you posted.

Her chest tightens.

The language feels familiar.

Too familiar.

She reads the messages again, slower this time.

Then the name appears deeper in the file.

Respondent: Daniel Harper — Social Worker

The name flickers somewhere in her memory.

Dan Harper.

But the thought refuses to settle. It would be an absurd coincidence. Surely there are dozens of Daniel Harpers in the city.

She flips ahead. The messages continue.

Sometimes it's easier to talk to a stranger.

Her stomach drops. She remembers typing that line.

Late at night.

On a burner phone.

She closes the file abruptly.

The room feels smaller now.

Sarah Harper arrives just before eleven. She looks younger than Erin expected. Late twenties, maybe. Her exhaustion sits plainly beneath her eyes. They shake hands.

Sarah sits forward in the chair as if ready to leave at any moment.

"I just want it to be over," she says.

Erin nods.

"You mentioned messages between your husband and the woman."

Sarah slides her phone across the desk.

"I forwarded them."

Erin scrolls carefully. The rhythm of the texts hits first.

Short sentences. Minimal punctuation. A careful distance.

Then one appears she remembers writing. The exact phrasing. A line she drafted twice before sending.

Her throat tightens.

Sarah keeps talking.

"He said it was a prank. One night. But the messages kept coming."

Erin forces her expression to remain calm.

"These are very clear," she says. "They'll be persuasive."

Sarah studies her face.

"Do you think the court will believe me?"

"Courts usually look for patterns," Erin replies evenly.

Sarah nods slowly. "I think I just want him to admit it. To say out loud that I'm not crazy."

She stares into her coffee.

"Do you ever get used to being lied to?"

Erin glances down at the printed messages.

One phrase stands out.

A sentence she remembers typing.

She lets the silence stretch.

"No," she says finally. "But people do get used to believing the simplest explanation."

Sarah frowns slightly.

"What do you mean?"

"In cases like this," Erin says carefully, "someone usually gets labeled the villain pretty quickly. Once that happens, it can be hard to see anything else."

Sarah nods.

"Yes. Exactly."

Erin closes the folder, her hand briefly covering the printed messages, suddenly self-conscious of the words on the page, before sliding the file back toward the center of the desk.

They finish the meeting quickly after that. When Sarah leaves, Erin remains seated. Her own words stare back at her from the printout as she tries to suppress a feeling of panic.

Back at her desk Erin enters the case into the firm's system.

Respondent: Daniel Harper

Occupation: Social Worker — Child Protective Services

The confirmation lands like cold water. There is no doubt now. Her fingers hover above the keyboard.

She opens the message log again. Every line carries the cadence of her own voice. She writes a neutral note in the file:

Further inquiry regarding third-party communications recommended.

Nothing more.

Across the hall someone laughs.

The office continues normally.

Erin stands and presses her forehead briefly against the glass window. The city outside is pale and distant. She wonders if her career is ending before it even began.

She sends Radcliffe a brief update email.

Then she returns to work.

Across town, Dan Harper is answering a call about a runaway teenager. He does not know a new attorney has taken his case. He does not know she once introduced herself as Misty.

Erin picks up the rubber dinosaur from behind her monitor and squeezes it until her pulse steadies. Then she sets it down and opens the next file.

Work continues.

Chapter Eleven

She doesn't look back. - Erin

Erin arrives forty-five minutes early.

The courthouse is all function; block walls, dim glass, fluorescent lights that flatten everything they touch. Above the entrance, the missing "J" in *Justice Center* leaves a faint outline in the stone, like something removed but not forgotten.

Inside, security moves people through without urgency. Shoes off. Bag open. Laptop out.

Erin waits her turn, then steps through. No one looks twice at her, which helps.

The waiting area is already half full. Bench seating lines the walls, and the low ceiling presses the noise into a steady hum. A vending machine glows in the corner, its contents unchanged from another decade.

She takes a seat near the wall and opens the Harper file. Not to learn anything new, just to steady herself.

Sarah's statement. The timeline. The messages.

Misty.

She reads a line, then another. Her own voice, flattened into evidence.

She closes the file.

Stay in the facts. Stay in control.

She checks the docket. Eight cases ahead of theirs.

Time stretches.

People shift, whisper, pace. A child kicks the leg of a chair in slow, rhythmic intervals. Someone's phone vibrates and is quickly silenced.

At 8:55, the bailiff appears.

"Courtroom B—first call."

Erin stands, gathers the file, smooths her jacket.

This is just another case.

She and Sarah take position near the courtroom doors. Sarah stands rigidly, her composure held together by effort alone. Her lipstick is precise, her posture too straight, like something braced for impact.

"Do you think he'll lie?" Sarah asks quietly.

"The court looks at evidence," Erin replies. "That's what matters."

Sarah nods, but her eyes don't settle.

"He's good at talking," she says. "People believe him."

Erin keeps her tone even. "That's why we stay focused."

A pause settles between them.

"You're very calm," Sarah says.

"That's my job. I spent a lot of time practicing these procedures."

The hallway fills around them, voices rising and falling, footsteps echoing, fragments of other people's crises passing in low conversation.

Erin scans the corridor without meaning to.

Looking.

Waiting.

Dan hasn't arrived.

Sarah checks her watch again. "He's late."

"He'll be here," Erin says.

Then movement catches at the far end of the hall.

He appears beside another attorney.

Erin sees him before she's ready.

Not his face at first, his posture. The way he carries himself, careful, contained.

Then his voice, low and measured.

And then his face. The recognition lands all at once.

It's him.

Her chest tightens, breath catching somewhere between inhale and release. For a moment, sound drops out entirely.

"That's him," Sarah whispers.

Erin nods.

"Yes." Her voice is steady. Her hands are not.

Dan doesn't look at them. He stays focused on his attorney, listening, nodding, contained in the way Erin remembers; controlled, deliberate, trying to keep everything from spilling over.

Erin lowers her gaze to the file.

You are not the story.

She doesn't look up again.

Inside, the courtroom fills quickly.

"All rise."

The judge enters, robes settling as she takes her seat. The room follows her movement, rising and sitting in practiced sequence.

"Harper versus Harper."

Erin stands.

"Erin Carter for the petitioner, Sarah Harper, present."

Opposing counsel introduces herself, then gestures to Dan.

"Daniel Harper, present."

Dan confirms procedural details when asked. His voice is unchanged; calm, measured, almost reassuring.

Erin keeps her eyes on her notes.

The hearing moves quickly. Disclosures confirmed. Assets mostly agreed. One issue remains unresolved.

When Dan speaks again, it is brief. "I'm not disputing the events," he says. "Only that they're being misunderstood."

The words land cleanly.

Too cleanly.

The judge nods, already moving forward.

"I'm ordering mediation within thirty days. If that fails, we'll set this for a contested hearing."

A pause, then:

"Try to resolve this."

The gavel taps lightly.

"Next case."

"All rise."

And just like that, it's over.

The room empties in a slow shuffle of relief and tension.

Sarah exhales, the sound unsteady. "That's it?"

"For now," Erin says. "Next step is mediation."

Sarah nods, but her expression doesn't soften.

"I just want him to admit it."

Erin says nothing.

After a moment, Sarah glances at her. "I saw you watching him."

"I was watching the room," Erin replies evenly.

Sarah studies her, then looks away.

"He always cared more about his work," she says. "More than anything else."

Erin closes the file. "People get pulled into things," she says. "Sometimes it looks different from the outside. Different understandings. I'm sure you guys have unresolved issues."

Sarah gives a small shrug. "Maybe."

They walk toward the exit together.

At the doors, Sarah pauses.

"Thank you," she says. "For believing me."

Erin holds her gaze for a fraction too long.

"You're welcome."

Sarah leaves.

Erin remains where she is. She then takes a deep breath.

The hallway is quieter now.

Erin stands alone, the file still in her hands.

She knows the truth.

Dan isn't what Sarah believes. The messages aren't what they appear to be. And she is the reason they exist.

Her thoughts move quickly, efficiently, like building a case against herself.

If she tells Sarah, she betrays her client.

If she tells the firm, she risks everything she's worked for.

If she says nothing, Dan carries the weight of a lie she helped create.

No option is clean.

Only damage.

She exhales slowly.

Maybe mediation fixes it. Maybe it settles quietly. Maybe no one looks too closely.

It's thin.

But it's something.

For now.

She turns toward the elevators and nearly walks straight into him.

Dan.

They both stop.

Too close.

He looks at her, really looks this time, his eyes narrowing slightly as something almost connects.

Recognition tries to surface.

Not quite there.

But close.

"Sorry," he says automatically.

Polite. Neutral.

Erin lowers her eyes. "Excuse me."

She steps past him without hesitation.

Doesn't stop. Doesn't turn.

Behind her, she can feel it, his attention lingering, trying to place her, trying to solve something just out of reach.

She keeps walking increasing her pace.

Out through the courthouse doors and into the cold air.

Only then does she breathe.

She doesn't look back.

She doesn't need to.

Chapter Twelve

"Suddenly everything makes sense and no sense at all." - Dan

Morning comes clean and unforgiving.

Erin steps onto the fourth floor, the firm already humming beneath glass and light. Everything here is controlled—angles, voices, posture. Even silence feels curated.

She reaches her office early. Too early. Again.

Inside, she moves through ritual: coat hung, desk aligned, monitor adjusted. Control in small things. It's the only kind available.

The Harper file waits.

She opens it, not to add, but to refine.

"Petitioner alleges infidelity…"

She edits without emotion. Strips tone. Replaces anything human with something safer. Words become distance. Distance becomes protection.

She skips the messages.

Her cursor hovers there, then moves on.

A notification appears.

Radcliffe: Quick check-in.

She composes her face and heads to his office.

Radcliffe doesn't look up right away.

"How's Harper?"

"Clean," Erin says. "They're pushing credibility, not facts."

He nods. "Good. Keep it that way. Pattern over incident. Judges like structure."

She nods.

"Don't give them anything messy."

"I won't."

He studies her a moment. "You're adjusting fast."

"I'm trying."

A faint smile. Approval, measured.

"Keep doing that."

Dismissed.

Back in her office, she exhales. She moves the file, one inch, then again.

Her thoughts settle into rhythm:

As long as no one looks closely, this holds.

She closes the file, locks it, and doesn't open the messages.

Outside, the city presses in.

Cold air. Wet pavement. Noise layered over noise.

Erin walks fast, not fleeing, but not lingering either.

A storefront stops her.

Mannequins in perfect suits. Clean lines. Belonging, manufactured.

Her reflection hovers in the glass is slightly off. Not quite right. Not quite them.

For a moment, she imagines stepping inside. Fixing it. Looking like a lawyer. Becoming what the firm expects.

Then—

What's the point if this falls apart? If she loses her job, she has failed. She can't help Jamie. She can't move on.

Her hand drops.

She turns away.

Across the street, a girl stands under a streetlamp, heels too high, skirt too short. The posture unmistakable.

Erin recognizes it instantly.

The performance. The calculation. The mask.

She looks away.

Keeps walking.

Night quiets everything, but not enough.

Erin sits on the floor, back against the futon, laptop closed. The apartment hums with small, failing sounds.

Her phone buzzes.

Unknown number.

u up?

Then—

Jamie

Her chest tightens.

Erin: *"Hey. I'm here. What's going on?"*

Jamie: *"Got in trouble for going to your graduation."*

She closes her eyes.

Erin: *"Did they hurt you?"*

Pause.

Jamie: *"No, just yelling. Sent me to my room."*

She exhales.

Erin: *"I'm glad. I was worried."*

Jamie: *"They didn't ask about you."*

That lands harder than expected.

Erin: *"No?"*

Jamie: *"Nope."*

Another pause.

Jamie: *"Things are still bad."*

She stares at the screen.

Erin: *"Worse?"*

Jamie: *"Just… louder."*

He tells her about food. About being forgotten. About walking home alone. About their mother taking his money. Le They also took his phone to keep him from texting Erin. How he hid a disposable phone.

Same house. Same patterns.

Nothing new. Nothing better.

Erin: *"I'll bring food soon."*

Jamie: *"Don't let her see."*

Erin: *"I won't."*

A pause.

Jamie: *"You looked like you belonged there."*

Her throat tightens.

Erin: *"You will too."*

Jamie: *"We'll see."*

Another pause.

Jamie: *"You're the only one I trust."*

She stares at the words.

Erin: "*You too. Always."*

The screen goes dark.

She doesn't move.

Just lies back on the floor, staring at the ceiling, listening to pipes.

Thinking—

You got out.

He didn't.

Sarah arrives early for the meeting with her attorney, Erin.

Too early.

She sits on the edge of the chair, bag clutched tight.

Erin enters, composed.

"Mediation is next," Erin says. "We'll walk through it."

Sarah nods, already unraveling.

"He's going to twist it. He always does."

"We'll stay with the facts."

"He's a social worker. He works with the courts sometimes. What if they believe him?"

"They won't decide. They facilitate."

Sarah lets out a breath that isn't relief.

"I just want him to admit it."

Erin pauses.

"That may not happen."

Sarah looks at her.

"I just don't want to be crazy."

"You're not."

The words come too easily.

They go through the process, step by step. Structure over emotion.

But Sarah keeps circling back.

"What if he makes it sound reasonable?"

Erin answers, but hears the truth underneath.

He *is* reasonable.

That's the problem.

At the door, Sarah hesitates.

"Do you believe me?"

Erin holds her gaze.

"Yes."

A lie. Or something close enough.

Sarah nods and leaves.

Erin sits alone.

The message tab glows on her screen.

She doesn't open it.

Mediation is about resolution.

Not truth.

The idea provides little comfort.

Dan's office is cluttered with lives.

Files stacked. Photos pinned. Kids frozen in time.

Jamie's file sits open.

Same pattern.

No proof. No action.

Just enough to worry. Not enough to intervene.

He rereads the notes; bruises, absences, food, silence.

Always silence.

He opens the message thread.

Misty.

Still no reply.

That's new.

He scrolls.

Reads again.

The language nags at him, too precise, too careful. Who is Misty? A neighbor? A family friend? Her texts read like formal reports for his file. She has insight into the family. Now silence.

Not random. Not casual.

He thinks of the bus stop.

Jamie looking away, too fast.

Dan closes the file.

Then opens it again.

Writes:

Home visit. Today.

The house is ready for him. Too ready. Clean. Still. Controlled.

Mr. Carter answers the door.

"You again."

"Just checking in."

Inside, everything staged. Nothing real.

Jamie sits on the couch.

Too still.

Hands folded. Eyes down.

Dan asks questions; school, food, routine.

Answers come fast.

Too fast.

The parents hover. Correct. Redirect. Control.

Dan watches, not what's said, but what isn't.

Jamie flinches once.

Small.

But enough.

Fifteen minutes.

Nothing actionable.

Everything wrong.

Dan stands to leave.

Then—

He sees the photo.

It's just a photo.

At first.

Jamie, younger.

And beside him, an older girl.

Her arm rests across his shoulder. Not posed. Not quite compliant. Like she stepped into the frame instead of being placed there.

There's something in her expression.

The eyes.

The angle of the chin.

Familiar.

Dan slows.

Then steps closer.

Studies it.

Something pulls at him. Not memory. Recognition.

Not fully formed, but there.

The hair. Dark in the photo.

The features. Controlled, even in something casual.

He's seen that face before.

He knows he has.

Before the thought can settle—

Mrs. Carter's voice comes from just behind him.

"That's our daughter," she says. "Jamie's sister."

Dan glances back briefly, then to the photo again.

"She's a lawyer now. Big firm downtown," she adds, a note of pride threaded with something sharper. "Got herself out. Doesn't come around much."

A lawyer.

The word lands.

Dan's gaze sharpens.

A courtroom.

A woman standing across from him.

Still posture. Controlled. Watching everything.

Sarah's attorney.

He looks back at the photo.

Really looks now.

The years begin to collapse. The structure of the face.

The eyes.

The set of the mouth.

It's close.

Too close.

His brow tightens slightly.

Dark hair.

but if it were lighter…

Blonde.

The thought hits before he can stop it.

And then—

the smile.

That same half-measured smile.

Careful. Contained.

Like every word is chosen before it's spoken.

Everything clicks.

The hotel. The voice. The messages.

Misty.

The room doesn't move, but the meaning of everything in it does.

Erin Carter.

Dan straightens just slightly, putting space between himself and the realization.

He keeps his face neutral.

Barely.

"Looks familiar," he says, controlled, almost offhand.

Mrs. Carter watches him for a beat, something flickering behind her expression, but she doesn't press.

"She always stood out," she says.

Dan nods once.

He doesn't ask anything else.

He doesn't need to. His mind is reeling. Things suddenly fall into place. His emotions are a mix of relief and fear at the same time.

On the way out, his fingers brush the edge of the frame, just once.

Cold glass.

Outside, the air feels sharper.

In the car, he sits still, phone already in his hand.

He opens the thread.

Misty.

The messages stare back at him, unchanged.

But now they mean something else entirely. Clearer. Suddenly everything makes sense and no sense at all.

He exhales slowly.

"Erin," he says under his breath.

Now he knows.

Everything just changed.

Chapter Thirteen

"If I do that…I lose everything." - Erin

The first hour of morning is always the purest: corridors empty, systems quiet, the illusion of control unchallenged by the sediment of the day. Erin sits at her desk, the light from the window casting a cold sheen across the glass, the HVAC humming with clinical precision.

She works methodically. The Harper file is open, its sections arranged like layers of injury. Each revision moves the document closer to something untouchable; tight, neutral, defensible. She edits in increments, never changing too much at once, always keeping the current version close enough to the last that no one can see the blood.

It needs updating after her meeting with Sarah.

She is midway through a sentence—*pattern of conduct… irreconcilable harm*—when the phone buzzes once.

She doesn't move at first.

Then she lifts the receiver.

"This is Carter."

"Reception. There's someone here to see you. Says it's urgent."

The tone is wrong. Too careful.

Erin glances at her calendar. Empty.

She stands, wipes her palms against the underside of the desk, smooths her skirt, and steps into the corridor. Her reflection follows her along the glass as if tethered.

She walks down to the lobby.

The receptionist doesn't speak, only glances toward the waiting area.

Dan Harper is sitting in the corner.

He looks… diminished. Cleaner than court, but worn down in a way that suggests long nights and no resolution. His hands are folded, but not in calm more like restraint.

Their eyes meet.

The impact is immediate.

"We shouldn't do this out here," Erin says.

He stands too quickly, as if pulled upright.

He follows her.

Neither speaks.

She closes the office door behind them, the latch clicking into place with quiet finality.

Outside, movement continues, shadows passing behind the glass, voices muffled into abstraction.

Inside, nothing moves.

Erin gestures to the chair.

Dan doesn't sit.

He scans the room; file, desk, window then settles on her.

"You're not what I expected," he says.

She lets the silence absorb it.

He steps toward the window.

"You were the one who called me," he says. "You were the one sending those messages."

"I'm not sure I know what you're talking about," she replies, but even she hears how thin it sounds.

He doesn't respond.

Instead, his gaze shifts, past her.

To a photo in her office on the desk behind her.

Erin sees it a second too late.

Her chest tightens. Not panic, something heavier. Final.

She closes her eyes briefly.

When she opens them, she knows.

He knows.

Dan doesn't rush it.

"I saw that photo," he says. "At the Carter house."

Erin doesn't move.

"Same one."

Silence.

"In court," he continues, "I thought I recognized you. Something was off."

He shakes his head.

"Then I reread the messages. Heard them in your voice."

Now he looks directly at her.

"You're her."

A beat.

"You're Misty."

The word lands without judgment.

Just fact.

Erin inhales slowly.

"Yes."

The room tightens around the truth.

She doesn't look away now.

"I'm not Misty. At least, not now. I was Misty."

There is no relief in saying it.

Only gravity.

"It started in law school," she says. "I couldn't afford to stay in. Loans weren't enough."

Dan says nothing.

"It wasn't supposed to last. Just long enough to finish." A pause. "I made sure no one could trace it. Different name. Wigs. Out-of-town clients."

Her voice steadies.

"You weren't supposed to matter."

That gets his attention.

"It was a setup," she says. "Your friends. A joke."

He flinches slightly.

"You didn't want anything," she continues. "You just… talked."

A beat.

"And I realized you cared."

Silence.

"About your work. About the kids."

Her voice tightens.

"And I thought you'd be the only one who would actually do something."

Now it comes faster.

"Jamie's not safe," she says. "He's never been safe."

Dan's posture shifts, engaged now.

"The house is controlled. Food is locked up. Everything is measured. He's learned how to survive inside it."

Her voice flattens, almost clinical.

"I grew up in that system. I know exactly what it is."

A beat.

"I left. Better yet, escaped."

That lands heavier.

"He didn't."

She looks at him directly now.

"So I used the only way in."

Silence.

"You."

Dan exhales slowly.

"You used me."

Not loud. Sharper that way.

Erin doesn't argue it.

"Yes."

That lands harder than denial would have.

Dan starts pacing.

"You built this," he says, gesturing toward the file. "You created this narrative."

"You think I had options?" she fires back.

"You had choices."

"So did you."

That stops him.

"You kept answering those messages."

"Because I thought I was helping a kid," he snaps.

"You were."

"And now I'm losing my wife because of it."

That lands.

Deep.

They stand in it.

No defense.

No easy correction.

Dan stops pacing.

The anger drains.

What's left is worse.

"I'm not here to expose you," he says.

Erin studies him.

"I need your help."

There it is.

Simple.

Clean.

Devastating.

"Tell her the truth," he says. "Tell Sarah what this actually was."

Erin doesn't respond immediately.

Her eyes flick to the file.

To the door.

To the glass.

"If I do that," she says carefully, "I lose everything."

"And if you don't," he replies, "I do."

Silence.

Balanced.

Impossible.

Erin finally moves.

Not away, but *into* it.

"Wait," she says.

Dan pauses.

She stands now, steadying herself against the desk.

"I need time."

"For what?" he asks.

"To fix it."

"That's not an answer."

"It's the only one I have right now."

He studies her.

"You've had months," he says.

"I didn't know you knew," she fires back. "I mean, I was hoping to fix it without anyone finding out about Misty."

A beat.

That lands.

She softens slightly, not weakness, but recalibration.

"If I walk into this wrong," she says, quieter now, "I don't just lose my job. I lose my license. My future. Everything I built to get my brother out. To give him a chance and not have to do the things I did to break free."

"And what do I lose?" he asks.

She doesn't answer.

Because she knows.

He presses.

"How much time?"

She hesitates.

"Tomorrow."

He almost laughs.

"That's not enough."

"It has to be."

He shakes his head.

"You're asking me to wait while my life collapses."

"I'm asking you to let me do this right," she says, sharper now. "If you force it, everything blows up. For both of us. We need each other's cooperation."

Silence.

He considers it.

"You tell me exactly what you're going to do," he says.

"I can't," she replies.

"That's not good enough."

"It's all I've got."

Another long beat.

Finally—

He nods.

Once.

Reluctant.

"Tomorrow," he says.

Not agreement.

A deadline.

He turns and leaves.

Chapter Fourteen

"who's dead, and what's the blackmail rate?" - Crystal

Night presses a band of black against the high windows of the office, rendering the glass walls more mirror than barrier. Erin sits in the exhausted glow of her desk lamp, the Harper file spread open in front of her like a crime scene, every page a fresh infraction. The office is quiet, the after-hours hush broken only by the intermittent pop of the HVAC and the sibilant slide of an elevator in the core. She is alone, or so she tells herself; in reality, the glass means she is always, potentially, observed.

She stares at the open file, but the lines on the page refuse to resolve into meaning. Her hands rest on the edge of the desk, fingers splayed, the right one trembling in a low, electrical way that does not stop when she presses it to the glass. The muscles in her neck refuse to loosen. Each breath is measured, shallow, a laboratory specimen of distress.

There is no plan for this. Every scenario in her head ends with some iteration of ruin: hers, Dan's, Sarah's. The logic engine that served her in law school and in every hustle before is stuck in an infinite recursion: Tell the truth and lose the only future she has ever built. Maintain the lie and watch Dan's marriage atomize under the weight of her own invention. There are no witness boxes here, no cross-examination, only a silent, unyielding jury composed of her own better selves.

On the other side of the glass, the corridors are deserted, but each reflective surface doubles her image, so that she is everywhere, infinite, a row of law firm cutouts lined up for inspection. She sees herself as she is: hair pulled too tight, eyes red where the concealer has failed, suit wrinkled from hours of inaction. And layered over that, the ghost of "Misty", the jawline gentled by a synthetic blonde curtain, the stance looser, the expression tuned to whatever the man across the hotel room required.

She closes the Harper file with a soft but absolute thump, the kind of sound that promises no further edits. Her left hand, steadier, finds the phone and draws it into the circle of lamplight. For three breaths, she holds it poised above the desk, as if the device were an artifact of enormous consequence.

She cannot confess. There is no version of that story which does not annihilate her: the internship, the first year, the license, the door to Jamie. If she comes clean, they will salt the earth behind her. She will be buried alive in ethics complaints and locked doors, a cautionary tale for every girl who ever thought she could game the system.

But the other option, the one where she says nothing, lets the Harpers wreck themselves on the reef of her own design, sits in her chest like an arrhythmic bomb. She feels the echo of Dan's voice, raw and unraveling: Tell her what really happened. Tell her why. She cannot bear it. She cannot bear that it is true.

There has to be another way.

Erin scrolls through her contacts, thumb navigating the alphabet with clinical detachment, until she lands on the name that does not belong in a lawyer's phone: Crystal. No last name. Just a memory of a girl in combat boots, who once said, "Don't look at the client. Look at their shoes. If you need to run, you'll know if you can outrun them." Crystal was always the backup plan.

She types: *"Need to see you. Tonight if possible. Urgent."*

She hovers, thumb poised over "Send." Her eyes flick to the glass walls, then to the dead black of the window, where her own face floats, ghosted by the city's sodium haze. In the double-image, she sees both Erin's at once, the one who built her life in the legal code, and the one who learned to survive by memorizing the weaknesses of others.

She presses send.

On the desk, the Harper file stares back at her, its pages now crowded into the clasp of the binder, the name "Sarah Harper" just visible under the tab. Erin moves with exaggerated care, collecting the file, tapping it square, then rising to her feet. The office is cold, and the ambient hum seems to amplify the sound of her own movements.

She crosses to the credenza, unlocks the top drawer with a coded flick, and slides the file inside. As she does, she scans the corridor outside, empty, but the after-image of her own movements lingers in the glass, a warning to stay invisible. She relocks the drawer, turns the key twice, and places it in her pocket. For good measure, she checks the lock again.

She returns to the desk and, unable to sit, stands by the chair with her arms crossed. She watches the phone for a response, every second swelling to a minute. At 10:19, the reply comes:

"Address? I can be there in 30."

She types the location of the building, no suite number, no name on the directory. They both know the rules. She deletes the text as soon as it's sent, then deletes the thread for good measure. She checks the outer office again: empty, the glass walls giving back only her own shape and the shape of the chair behind her, the one Dan had occupied that morning.

The silence begins to ferment, sour and strange. She paces the length of the office, three steps each way, then stands at the window, hands pressed to the glass. Below, the city is a logic puzzle of headlights and stoplights, every car a witness to something it does not understand.

She thinks: There is no solving this. There is only surviving it. She glances at the phone, willing it to stay silent. Then, as if summoned, the device blinks with a new message. *"Outside. Call when ready."*

She keys in the main entrance code, then waits at her desk, the phone facedown this time, the tremor in her right hand now a full-body phenomenon. She counts the seconds, feeling them accumulate in the hollow behind her ribs.

In the glass, her reflection holds the pose: a woman in a suit, hair tight, mouth set to "war." Behind her, the door of the office is ajar, the corridor a tunnel of potential exposure.

She wonders, for a split second, if there is a word for this moment: the second before the house collapses, the breath before the first domino falls.

She decides there must be.

She waits for the knock, knowing it is already too late to run.

The knock comes soft but urgent, a rap that knows both its own importance and the rules of discretion. Erin crosses to the door, opens it just enough for a glimpse. Crystal stands on the threshold in black jeans and a jacket whose ancestry is half biker, half tactical vest. Her hair is up, streaked platinum at the ends, and she wears an expression of permanent, amused suspicion. The security lights cast her in a film-noir chiaroscuro, and for a moment, Erin flashes back to the grim apartments and after-hours meetups of another life.

Crystal glances up and down the corridor, then ducks in fast, moving with a precision born of both paranoia and intent. "Nice digs," she whispers, eyes sweeping the empty outer offices, then up at the camera above the entry. "Guess they finally let you join the cult, huh?"

Erin says nothing, just closes the door and sets the lock. She gestures for Crystal to follow, leads her down the hall past the paralegal bullpen and the wall of photos, each one a glamour-shot of partner triumph and into her own office. The door closes with a pneumatic sigh. Erin draws the vertical blinds tight, the slats stuttering closed like a zipper. It is now just the two of them, the room insulated against everything but the past.

Crystal flops into the visitor chair, then immediately pivots, boot up on the knee, surveying the landscape. "Shit, Carter. I almost didn't recognize you. You look…" She trails off, groping for a word that covers the transformation without making it sound like a compliment. "...expensive."

Erin does not smile. She returns to her desk, stays standing behind it, as if the three feet of wood and glass could buffer whatever this is about to become.

"So," Crystal says, lacing her fingers behind her head, "who's dead, and what's the blackmail rate?"

Erin feels the line between her teeth, as if she is biting down on a string that could unravel everything. "You ever hear of a guy named Dan Harper?" she asks.

Crystal snorts. "The Social worker you told me about once, right? Real charity-case look. Helping you with your brother. Why?"

"He was a client," Erin says, careful, "but not really. It was a prank. His coworkers booked me for a conference, but he didn't go through with it. He just wanted to talk. Now his wife wants a divorce and he figured out it was me."

Crystal's eyes widen a notch, then narrow. "So you got a Good Samaritan in a sling over nothing. That's classic." She shifts forward, more alert now, elbows on knees. "He making trouble?"

Erin shakes her head. "He came to me. Said he'd keep it quiet, but he wants his wife to believe the truth. He wants me to talk to her, convince her he didn't…" She breaks off, the words too gross, too technical. "..that it wasn't what she thinks."

"Ok, minor problem," Crystal shrugs.

"There's another problem," Erin says.

Crystal rolls her eyes as Erin continues. "I was assigned to the wife's divorce case."

"As her lawyer?" Crystal says. "Damn Erin."

Crystal whistles, low and tuneful. "You want me to play Misty for the wife. You want me to be you. To bail you and the knight out of this thing."

Erin nods, once, the admission a small defeat.

"That's some fuckin' white-knight shit, right there," Crystal says, but she grins as she says it. She cocks her head, calculating the angles. "What's the endgame?"

Erin's hands grip the edge of the desk, but she keeps her voice steady. "I want you to meet her. Say it was you that night, that nothing happened. Say the whole thing was a prank, just like he told her. Which is the truth. Then disappear."

Crystal leans back, rocking the chair onto two legs. "You want me to risk perjuring myself, maybe get a beating from a pissed-off spouse, just to keep your shiny new job safe?"

"I'll pay," Erin says, the word so hard-edged it clangs against the glass walls.

Crystal waves it off. "I know you will. It's not the money. It's the logistics." She drums her fingers, eyes flicking to the door, the blinds, the perimeter. "You realize, if this blows back, it's not just you on the line. I've got priors, Carter. I can't be in the news."

Erin's jaw sets. "No one will know. It's a one-time thing. You meet her, you say the script, you're gone."

"And you're sure she'll buy it? You sure Harper's not setting you up for a sting?"

Erin shakes her head. "He's desperate. He hates this. He's also straight as an arrow. He just wants it to end."

Crystal studies her for a long moment, then shrugs. "I'll need the details. The story. And a good enough alibi if anyone looks too close."

Erin slides a legal pad across the desk, flips to a blank page. "I wrote out the sequence. Where it happened, what we talked about. You just need to remember the basics: hotel, conference, the way the room looked. There's no video, no photos. His wife only has messages, and I already burned the number."

Crystal picks up the pad, scans the page, then glances up. "You thought this all out."

"It's my job," Erin says, the phrase bitter as old metal.

Crystal smirks, but the admiration is real this time. "Guess you really did make it out."

Erin wants to say, "Nobody ever makes it out," but instead she stays still, letting the tension in the room soak through the air.

Crystal tosses the pad down, then stands. She crosses to the window, tugs one slat open with a pinkie, surveys the night. "So when do I meet her?"

"I'll set it up," Erin says. "You'll get the script by tomorrow. You'll get paid the day after."

Crystal turns, eyes sharp. "This is the last time, right? No more calls? No more skeletons?"

Erin nods, her mouth a hard, straight line.

Crystal smiles, all canines and mischief. "It's a hell of a story, Carter. You ever write a book, leave my name out of it."

Erin relaxes, a breath escaping, but she does not smile.

Crystal moves toward the door, pausing with her hand on the knob. "Hey," she says, voice softer now. "Whatever you did to get here, I get it. You don't owe me an apology."

Erin meets her gaze, holds it, and nods once.

Crystal slips out, quiet as she came. The door clicks shut, leaving Erin in the soft, institutional darkness. She stands, back to the window, and feels the new weight settling onto her shoulders.

The plan is set. The dominoes are in motion.

All she has to do now is survive the aftermath.

The next day, before the city's grid has time to warm under the sunrise, Erin waits in the shadow of the conference room with her arsenal laid out: legal pads, a Sharpie, two burner phones, and a manila envelope so thick it barely fits her purse. She has not slept. Instead, she's spent the night cycling through every line of attack, every counter, every conceivable slip in the story they are about to manufacture.

Crystal arrives on the dot, hair still damp from the shower, a duffel bag slung over one shoulder. She smells faintly of hotel shampoo and whatever coffee she has managed to commandeer from the lobby. She moves with the briskness of someone who has never once been late to her own disaster.

Erin lets her in, then closes the blinds and sits. Crystal scans the table, then the perimeter. "You expecting a wire?" she says, half-joking, but her eyes keep moving, logging exits and weak spots.

"I don't take chances," Erin says, but her voice comes out thinner than intended.

"Good," Crystal says, dropping into the chair opposite. "Neither do I."

They get right to it. Erin opens a pad, draws a flowchart: "Point A—Sarah Harper. Point B—Misty, a.k.a. you. Point C—total exoneration of Harper." She underlines "total" three times. She narrates as she writes, each word precise: "We meet at Cafe Republic, a block off the courthouse. You arrive first, take a window seat. I'll text you when Sarah's inbound."

Crystal nods, already working the scenario. "And the story?"

Erin slides a single page of handwritten notes across the table. "You confirm you were hired by the coworkers, not Dan. You say he refused all services, talk only. You say you left after twenty minutes, and the rest was just paperwork and a follow-up call about a kid in his caseload. I've drafted a script. Stick to the script."

Crystal scans the notes, lips moving as she runs through the lines. "She'll ask what we talked about. Why it went on for so long."

Erin anticipated this. "You tell her he was venting about his job, how he couldn't help all the kids who needed him. You say he mentioned his wife, said he loved her but didn't know how to help her trust him. You get emotional, make her feel like you're the one who's sad for them. He was helping out a client for you. A kid in trouble. After the hotel it was all social work business. And all that is the truth."

Crystal's eyebrow arches, admiring. "You were always good at this."

"Not good enough," Erin says.

"Don't beat yourself up. Nobody could've kept the double act going forever."

They get granular. Erin runs her through the physical details: the room number at the hotel ("707—never forget a double-oh-seven"), the furniture ("square table, coffee pot, mismatched glasses from catering, no mini-bar"), the ambient sounds ("He played a sleep app on his phone, rainforest noises"). They rehearse Sarah's likely questions, the tone of her voice, the way she will try to trip up a liar. Crystal has to be both credible and forgettable, memorable enough to be believed, bland enough to never be traced.

"If she asks for proof?" Crystal says, twirling a pen.

"You say the agency doesn't keep records. You got paid in cash. You never saw Dan after the conference, not once."

Crystal leans back, lips pursed. "You really think she'll drop the case after this?"

Erin shakes her head. "I think it's the best shot we've got. If not, we reset."

Crystal watches her, a long, speculative look. "You used to have a plan for everything. Always a parachute."

"Still do," Erin says, but it sounds less like a boast than a warning.

Crystal cracks her knuckles, picks up the page again. "She's gonna grill me. I can feel it. You want me to cry, or just keep it dry?"

"Read the room," Erin says. "But if you can cry, do. That's gold."

"Yeah," Crystal says, mouth twitching at the corners. "All right. Let's run it."

They rehearse: Erin playing the role of the suspicious wife, Crystal morphing between meek, dismissive, and wounded. The first attempt is a mess, Crystal goes too hard, tries to sell herself as a therapist, gets the timeline wrong. Erin calls her on it, and they start over.

The second run is better. Crystal hits all the talking points, and when Erin pounces with, "Why did he keep texting you if nothing happened?" Crystal shoots back, "He's throws himself into his work. It was all about the kid client after that." It is perfect. Erin marks it on the pad with a star.

After an hour, Crystal has the script down cold. Erin's relief is visible, a loosening in the jaw, a slackening of the death grip on her pen.

"You're the best," she says, and for a second, it almost feels like old times.

"Of course I am," Crystal says. She takes a last scan of the notes, then tucks the page into her jacket. "When do you want to roll?"

Erin glances at the clock. "Tonight. I already told Sarah you'd be there."

Crystal's smile is feline, all teeth and anticipation. "Goddamn, you don't waste time."

Erin stands, walks to the window. The city is awake now, the office towers shedding light into the street like so many searchlights. She feels the familiar tug of anxiety, but also the strange calm of having engineered the most likely outcome.

She returns to the desk, pulls out the manila envelope. The weight of it is tangible, a semester's rent, maybe two. She slides it across the table, and Crystal scoops it up without fanfare, not even a flicker of greed.

She stands, slings her bag over her shoulder. "Last thing," she says. "What if this isn't the end of it? What if she finds another thread to pull?"

Erin's eyes go cold. "Then you and I are never in the same room again. Ever."

Crystal nods, the game understood. She tucks the envelope into her bag, then steps around the table. She gives Erin a hug.

"Don't let them eat you alive, Carter. That's what they do. That's all they do."

Erin nods, unable to speak. The world is suddenly too sharp.

Crystal turns to leave, pauses at the door. "Hey," she says, voice softer. "He's just a guy. Don't make yourself a ghost for him."

Erin shakes her head. "It's not him."

Crystal's eyes crinkle, a puzzle solved. "It's Jamie, isn't it? It's always Jamie."

Erin lets out a shaky breath. "He's the only thing that matters."

Crystal grins, then leaves without another word. The room is filled with the throb of the city, the ache of the future pressing in.

Erin sits back in her chair, stares at the empty space where Crystal was, and allows herself one minute to believe she's bought them both another chance.

Then she gets up, smooths her skirt, and walks out, the plan in place, the aftermath already coming.

Chapter Fifteen

"That would be the greatest injustice, to get blamed for something you never did." - Erin

The law library at Stein-Radcliffe is built to intimidate, a gallery of glass slabs, expansive, mirrored steel, and books so surgically curated they may as well be props. The architecture is all reveal and surveillance: double-height ceilings, inner offices exposed by their own dioramic transparency, the long central table a runway of unsparing light. Every surface is a cold alloy, polished, planar, utterly resistant to comfort.

Erin enters first, as planned, her suit pressed to an apology, every gesture measured for plausible deniability. The glass doors don't squeak, they hiss, and the echo follows her to the central table, where she sets down a single folder and composes herself at the head, as if chairing an invisible tribunal. She has thirty-seven seconds before Sarah arrives, a margin calculated to allow for the possibility of doubt, but not enough to encourage escape.

The bench seats are empty, the only witness a resin sculpture of Lady Justice holding her scales at a traffic-cam angle. Erin wipes a phantom smudge from the tabletop, then positions the folder so its label faces her, not the room: HARPER, SARAH V. HARPER, DANIEL.

When Sarah arrives, she is not the woman of the corridor, not the desperate petitioner who'd clung to every syllable in pretrial. Here, she is more condensed, her features rigid, the jawline sharper than memory. She wears her coat open over a gray wool dress, her shoes low, hair pulled back in a way that would have read "careless" if the rest of her were not so armored.

Erin stands, smoothing the lapel, and greets her with the exact handshake she would give a hostile witness: brisk, unyielding, but technically courteous.

Sarah says nothing at first. She sits and arranges her tote at her feet, then levels her gaze at the ceiling-high bookshelves, as if searching for a precedent in the nearly empty large law library. The silence grows not awkward but ceremonial, a protocol in itself.

"We're still on for mediation tomorrow," Erin begins, voice pitched low and even. "But I wanted to give you a chance to hear something that may affect your position from the person best positioned to get some insight."

Sarah's eyebrows flick, then settle. "About meeting Misty?"

"Yes." Erin slides the folder across the table but does not open it. "As we discussed, she is a third party willing to provide context. She's agreed to meet with you, just for a few minutes. You don't have to say anything, and you can leave whenever you want."

Sarah leans back, arms crossed but relaxed, the posture of someone who expects an ambush but also craves it. "Fine."

"Just hear her out. I'll be at the far end of the library, if you need anything. You're not alone." Erin keeps the words as neutral as possible, a soft landing for what comes next.

Sarah almost smiles. "You make it sound like I'm about to meet a ghost."

Erin catches the thread of old sarcasm and tucks it away. "Again, just hear her out. That's all I ask."

Sarah nods once, eyes flaring with the micro expression of someone who has already written the script of disappointment, but is prepared to be surprised.

Erin stands, steps away from the table, and takes up a post at a smaller desk near the library's east wall. From here, she can see every angle but cannot hear specifics. She removes a legal pad, uncaps a pen, and writes "Mediation prep—Harper" at the top, as if it were any other task. Her hands, beneath the glass of the side table, press flat to her thighs. She is hyperaware of her own stillness, the precise way she must occupy the space: visible but not intrusive, present but not party.

In her head, the phrase repeats: This should work. This has to work.

The lights overhead are fluorescent but tuned to simulate daylight; the effect, at this hour, is monstrous. Every imperfection is magnified, every motion given a double shadow. The only relief comes from the frosted side panels, which catch the late morning and refract it into sterile rainbows on the marble floor. Erin fixates on these chromatic errors, lets them distract her from the shudder of anticipation in her bones.

She checks the time: 11:59. Crystal will be punctual.

Across the table, Sarah has not moved. She sits, hands folded over one knee, expression neutral but for the tension in the line from temple to jaw. The meeting is so tightly wound that when the side door opens, noiseless, a trick of the hydraulics, both women register the arrival with only a flick of their eyes.

Crystal enters, disguised as Misty, the platinum wig so precisely aligned that for an instant Erin feels the vertigo of seeing her own erased history rendered in three dimensions. Crystal's clothes are simple, dark jeans, gray pullover, black boots, but her walk is a deliberate echo of the persona: a touch more swing in the hips, a softness in the shoulders, the hands kept visible at all times.

She crosses to the central table and sits opposite Sarah without waiting to be invited. She removes a phone from her pocket but does not check it, placing it screen-down on the glass.

The two women study each other. The silence is glacial, but there is none of the raw volatility that might have threatened an earlier, less engineered encounter.

Erin can hear bits and pieces, but she does not need to. She reads the scene in body language: the way Crystal inclines her head, never meeting

Sarah's gaze except for measured, plausible moments; the way Sarah sits a fraction higher, like a diver preparing for a very cold pool. Erin notes, too, the flex of Crystal's jaw, the infinitesimal delay before she responds to the first question, she's in character, but the stakes are higher than Erin can signal from her perch.

This should work. This has to work.

Crystal, as Misty, opens with a calibrated version of the script voice two clicks below natural, posture tuned for minimal threat, every word wrapped in the Midwestern affect that neither of them owns but both understand as currency. She introduces herself as Misty. She says she remembers the hotel room, the conference badge, the awkward first minute when neither party seemed to want to be the client. "He just wanted to talk," she says, the phrase recited with the practiced care of someone repeating a detail from a script, but with just enough emphasis to suggest authenticity.

Sarah does not blink for the first three sentences. She sits with her forearms flat on the glass, hands folded but not relaxed, eyes trained not on her face but on the spot just to the left of it, as if using peripheral vision to search for edges. Her first response is a question, not an acceptance: "Why did you keep messaging him after the fact?"

Crystal smiles, the motion designed to signal self-deprecation. "He was authentic. Loves his job and I needed help for my brother."

Sarah's mouth forms a line so tight it could split granite. She says, "The messages sounded cryptic."

Crystal shakes her head. "That's not how I meant it. I just, some people want to know there's no record. I also knew I was imposing on his job as a social worker." She laughs, too sharp, then corrects the smile. "Really."

Erin, from her vantage at the auxiliary table, sees the correction, notes the excess. She can tell that Crystal is overcompensating: the hands fidget too often, the eye contact is a hair too fixed, the transitions between points are too practiced. It isn't so much what Crystal is saying but how she says it. This is not the effortless con of old, it's a performance frayed by the magnitude of the stakes.

Sarah leans in, folding the space between them. "The hotel says you checked in under a different name," she says, voice almost kind. "They said you were wearing a wig."

Crystal nods, as if relieved to change the angle. "Yeah, agency policy. Protects the girls. And some guys like the fantasy, you know?" She tilts her head, lets the wig's synthetic hair catch the fluorescent light, a flicker of the old burlesque. "It's all make-believe. Safer for everyone." She lets out a nervous laugh.

Sarah's fingers, now untwined, begin to drum a complex rhythm on the glass. She says, "He never mentioned you. Not once, after the conference. I overheard his friends talking." The words have the force of an accusation but none of the heat. "So why are you telling me this now?"

Crystal's eyes dart, just for a fraction, to the side, toward where Erin sits, out of the direct line of fire but visible enough to offer silent support. She says, "I heard you were divorcing. Sometimes that happens when the truth is left out too long. I thought maybe it would help if you heard it from me. So you'd know he wasn't a monster."

Erin's breath is shallow; she counts it against the faint click of Sarah's nails. She knows this tempo: the rising edge of interrogation, the way the witness starts with questions and then, bit by bit, takes control of the room.

Sarah leans back, breaking the tension, but instead of softening she grows more precise. "Why are you protecting him?" she asks, and it lands with the force of a challenge. "If it was just business, why are you here now?"

Crystal's answer is slower now, less assured. "He was nice," she says, the word almost foreign in her mouth. "That's all. Most aren't." She looks down, then up again, hands flat on the table. "Look, I don't know what you need to hear from me. I was paid to show up, he talked, I left. I haven't seen him since."

Sarah's gaze becomes a metronome: left, right, then fixed on Crystal. The next question is softer, almost whispered: "Was there anything else? Anything that would make him want to keep it secret?"

Erin can feel the static charge from across the room; she imagines the air filled with hairline fractures, every word a fresh vector for disaster.

Crystal says, "No. I swear. I mean, he seemed more interested in talking about his work. I guess he has confidentiality he has to abide by." She shrugs, and this time the gesture is perfect, a resignation that cannot be faked.

Sarah's eyes shift, uncertainty breaking through the surface. She says, "He always said he was trying to save people. Even when it hurt us." The admission comes out as if by accident, an old wound showing through the sleeve. "I thought he just wanted out. An excuse."

The silence after this is long, and heavy, and Erin feels the weight of it pinning her to the chair. She allows herself to believe, for a moment, that the plan is working: the decoy is holding, the narrative is aligning, and the whole mess will resolve without additional bloodshed.

But Sarah is not finished.

She says, "You know we can check this with Dan. I told him I was meeting you."

Crystal blinks, the first true break in the armor. Erin, from her seat, sees the same secondhand: the stutter in Crystal's hands, the way her shoulders hunch, the way she tries to recover the thread of the script and cannot.

Across the room, Erin freezes, coffee cup raised halfway to her mouth. Her vision tunnels, her pulse surges in her throat. She had not planned for this. She had not even considered it.

Sarah repeats, "He said he wanted to talk to you himself. He thought meeting you was a good idea."

Crystal looks down, mouth tight. "I don't think that's a good idea," she says, her voice flat.

"Why not?" Sarah says, and the tone is not curiosity but triumph, the satisfaction of having found the fracture line. "We can settle it before mediation tomorrow."

Crystal hesitates, then says, "Sometimes people don't want to remember. That's all."

Sarah looks at her watch. He said he'd be late. But said since you and I already knew each other that he thought he'd give us a few moments anyway before he arrived. He should be here any minute. "Wonder why he said that?"

Erin noticed Crystals face. It was like a mouse caught in a trap. All Erin heard was "Dan". Then she looks toward the door and her breath catches in her throat.

The sound of the library door opening is a small event, barely enough to register against the hum of the lights, but it detonates in Erin's chest with all the force of a fire alarm. She cannot move at first, every muscle not in her control, her jaw locked around the phrase "This is not happening, this is not happening." She tries to lower her eyes, but they are already down; she tries to hide her face so that he doesn't see her as he enters.

Dan enters with the hesitancy of someone who expects to be unwelcomed, a loose-shouldered, slouching trajectory that suggests he would much rather be invisible. He scans the room, gaze sweeping the tables in a motion that lands, with pinpoint accuracy, on Sarah.

She turns at his approach. "Hey," she says, and the greeting is so stripped of affect it could be a line from a play, one that has been workshopped into meaninglessness. Dan stands a good five feet away, like he's wary of an invisible perimeter.

Erin's body tries to make itself smaller across the room, shoulders tightening, neck retracting, knees drawn in. Her hands are flat on her thighs, the skin numb from pressure. She tries to make herself invisible.

Dan glances briefly past Sarah, searching for someone else. "Where's Erin?" he says, as if checking for a missing item on a receipt.

Sarah blinks, once, twice, and then tilts her head. "You mean Misty?" she says, confusion reshaping the lines of her face. "I'm meeting with Misty, not Erin."

Dan stares at her, then at Crystal, the wig's synthetic shine rendered grotesque by the daylight shining through the window framing everything as if in a celestial moment. For a second, Dan's eyes flick from Crystal to Sarah. The room is a closed loop of misrecognition and mounting panic.

Crystal says nothing. Her eyes dart, quicksilver, between the three of them, then settle on Erin across the room with a plea so naked it could be a scream.

Sarah, picking up on the confusion, says to Dan, "I just heard her side. You said you didn't mind if I talked to her first."

Dan's voice is almost a whisper, but it carries. "That's not Misty," he says, pointing at Crystal. "Where's Erin?"

For a moment, nobody breathes.

Crystal straightens, adopts the old brashness, but her voice is brittle as meringue. "I told you already, it was a one-time thing. If you don't remember, that's your problem."

Sarah looks at Dan, then back to Dan. "You said she would explain. That it would make sense if I talked to her."

Dan says, "Yes, but I'm confused. I thought you were meeting with Erin."

"No." Sarah says. "Misty".

"Who is this?" Dan says.

Erin forces herself to breathe. She stands, slowly, as if moving through molasses, and walks across the library floor, the click of her shoes a metronome of defeat.

She stops at the edge of the central table, close enough that the fluorescent bulbs cast sharp shadows under her eyes.

"I guess I need to explain," she says, and the words taste like bleach.

Nobody speaks. The silence is perfect, crystalline. Erin looks at the faces before her: Sarah's, searching and hurt; Dan's, guarded but not surprised; Crystal's, hardening into its old space.

She draws a breath, lets it out.

"I'm Misty," she says, and the truth lands without an echo. The room is all glass, all exposure, and there is nowhere left to hide.

Erin stands at the edge of the table, wrists visible, chin upright, as if entering a witness box for her own trial. For a moment no one blinks, not even Crystal, whose usual reflex for spectacle has failed her. The air is thick with aftershock.

"I'm Misty," Erin repeats, her voice neither loud nor apologetic, just atomically precise. "Or I was. It was a job. I never planned for it to matter."

She looks at Sarah, then at Dan, then at the space between them, a gap charged with all the words she hasn't yet found the courage to say.

"I put myself through law school," she says, the words coming in short, clean cuts. "The loans were never enough. My parents gave up on me, and I had a little brother to support. Every month was an equation that didn't work. So I found a way." She gestures at her own hair, now a sober brown, at the tailored suit that says nothing about the life underneath. "I wore a blonde wig. Used a fake name. Saw men who wanted to be invisible as much as I did."

She looks at Dan. "The night your friends booked me, I didn't even want to go. But the agency was short, and you looked safe. Like you'd be the easiest hour of my life."

Dan holds her gaze, blinking slow. He says nothing.

"I went to your room," Erin says. "You were nervous. You told me right away you didn't call. We figured out your friends were playing a joke. You just wanted to talk or I wanted to talk when I found out you were a social worker." She pauses, remembering the careful awkwardness of his hands, the way he made sure the door stayed open a crack. "We sat on opposite sides of the couch. You talked about your job. About the kids, the cases, the ones you lost sleep over. You told me about Sarah. You said she was smarter than you and you were nervous about the joke. I needed a contact with child protective services, figured fate put us together."

A silence follows, huge and articulate.

Erin goes on, voice hardening as the adrenaline kicks in. She looks at Sarah. "I left after thirty-seven minutes. That's the truth. I never saw him again, until court. I didn't even recognize him at first. I panicked when I realized what was happening."

She turns to Crystal. "She's a friend. When I realized my career was on the line, that this could all explode, I asked her to help. To pretend to be me, for one hour, to keep everything from falling apart." She looks at Sarah, bracing for the reaction. "It was a mistake. I shouldn't have done it. When Dan learned I was Misty, it was all I could think of to try to make things right. For everyone."

Sarah stares, jaw locked.

Erin reaches for the center, the core that matters. "My brother, Jamie, is thirteen now. He's smart, and funny, and a million times kinder than me. But his home isn't safe. I tried every way I could think of to get him out; filed reports, called in favors, even tried to get guardianship. But the system doesn't work unless there's blood, or drugs, or something you can measure."

She closes her eyes for one second, then opens them.

"Dan, you took him on as his caseworker after our first and only meeting. You said you cared about the kids nobody else did. I thought if I could get your attention, maybe you'd see him. Maybe you'd help."

She looks at her hands, splayed on the table. "That's why I did it. All of it."

Crystal, uncharacteristically, says nothing. Even her breathing is held in abeyance.

Erin lifts her head, lets the tension burn away every last layer of pretense. "This is my first case as a lawyer. And it's over now. I know that."

She addresses Sarah directly, her voice both confession and plea. "You deserve the truth. Dan didn't cheat. He didn't even try. I lied to save myself. But I can't let him lose you for something he didn't do. That would be the greatest injustice, to get blamed for something you never did. I can't think of anything worse."

The fluorescent lights catch a shine on the tears that do not fall. Erin's shoulders drop, and her voice goes quiet.

"I just hate injustice," she says. "That's why I became a lawyer. But today, I'm the one who's guilty."

The silence is so complete it's almost holy.

For a second, the room is nothing but light and breath and the slow, seismic shift of what can never be restored.

The aftermath is a stasis, as if the confession has forced every atom in the room to recalibrate its place in the universe. Even the air seems thicker, more viscous; the HVAC's white noise now a concrete pressure against the eardrums. Erin is aware of her own breathing, the way each exhale trembles at the finish.

Dan stands very still, hands buried in his pockets, shoulders slightly caved. The hurt is visible in the shallow lines around his mouth and eyes, deepened in a way that is more testament than accusation, but his chin remains up, his posture resisting collapse. He stares at Sarah, and for a second, every muscle in his face seems to pulse with the desire to reach her, but he remains anchored.

He says, softly, "I told you the truth." No drama, just the line itself, offered like a coin to be accepted or not.

Sarah lowers herself into a chair, sits with her knees locked together, elbows planted on the edge of the glass table. She does not look at anyone. Her fingers draw slow, involuntary spirals on the surface, as if mapping the ruins of her own certainty. It is a while before she speaks.

When she finally looks up, it is at Dan. Her face is absent of anger, but full of something more complicated, a layering of old wounds and new calculations. She searches his eyes, not for a lie, but for some evidence that she could have been wrong all along.

Sarah shifts her gaze to Erin, and in the moment of contact, the current of emotion is so sharp that Erin has to look down.

No one moves for a long time.

Erin becomes aware of the weightlessness in her hands, the float of her own pulse, the way her knees have lost all resistance. She feels as if she has been flayed, every nerve exposed to the ambient light.

Sarah's breathing, once quick and shallow, now slows. Her hands stop moving. She says, almost to herself, "So that's it."

Dan doesn't answer. He waits.

Sarah's eyes go back to him. The wariness is gone, replaced by something like mourning, or relief. She says, "You really didn't touch her."

"No," says Dan. The word is smaller than the space it fills.

Sarah looks at the table, then at her own hands, then at him again.

The edges of the world start to soften. The expectation of violence, the psychic kind, begins to fade. In its place is a hollowness, but not an empty one.

Sarah's shoulders relax. She sits a bit taller, as if a burden has been removed, though she does not know where it went.

All at once, the three of them are reconfigured: no longer adversaries, not quite allies, just survivors in the sudden hush of aftermath.

Sarah is the one who finally speaks. "You didn't cheat," she says, and the words do not rise as a question but fall with the force of a sentence. "You really didn't. You were just helping with her brother the whole time."

Dan nods once, hands still deep in his pockets. He looks older than he did twenty minutes ago, but also less haunted.

Sarah opens the folder on the table, takes out the divorce petition, and looks at it as if seeing a relic from a vanished civilization. She folds it in half, then in half again, and slides it back into the manila. "I'm not moving forward with this," she says. "Not now." She glances at Dan, and there is a tremor of irony in her voice. "We're not completely okay, because his work over shadows our marriage. But If he's willing to let's work on it…"she lets the question hang.

Dan manages a smile. "I throw myself into work. It's a problem. Yes, we can work on it. Together."

Sarah almost laughs. "I know. I think I married you for that." She lets the words rest, not trying to fill the space.

He says, "I can try to fix it. I want to."

Sarah nods, then turns to Erin.

"You should help her," she says to Dan, with a tilt of her head. "She risked everything to do the right thing. Even if it meant blowing up her own future."

Erin blinks, stunned by the generosity, by the clarity of the verdict. "I didn't—" she starts, then lets the protest die.

Sarah's mouth curves at the edges. "You'll be a great lawyer," she says. "Risking your career for justice? That's what they all say at the interviews, but nobody actually does it. I'm dropping the divorce. I guess you can tell your boss you handled it." Sarah then smiles.

For a second, Erin can't speak. She grips the edge of the table, grounding herself. The old feeling of being caught, of being measured and found wanting has been replaced by something alien: a lightness, almost a vertigo.

Sarah stands, collects her bag, and looks at Dan. "Let's go home." He nods, and together they walk out, side by side her hand reaching for his as he takes her hand.

Erin looks down at her hands, then up at the space where the couple had stood, and for the first time in months, she does not feel afraid.

Crystal is the one who punctures the silence, as always.

"So… do I need to give the money back?" she says, eyebrow raised, voice perfectly even. The line floats above the wreckage, absurd and entirely logical.

Dan, halfway through the doors with Sarah, stops, blinks, as if the question had to travel through three dimensions before reaching him.

Sarah's lips twitch, and though it never becomes a full smile, the movement is unmistakable: the first signal of levity since they entered the room.

Erin, standing by the table, lets her exhaustion surface. She doesn't try to hide it. She reaches up and runs a hand through her hair, the dark, real hair, not the manufactured persona and lets her shoulders round, for once not worrying about who might be watching.

The question hangs a moment, then dissolves into a laughter so dry and brief it hardly qualifies, but is real all the same.

For the first time, Erin looks at Crystal and smiles back. "Keep it," she says, and the words are lighter than she would have believed possible.

The two of them stand in the afterimage of what just happened, and for a moment, everything is simple: the truth out, the money spent, the story closed.

The glass walls are as transparent as ever, but now, they feel like windows, not cells.

Chapter Sixteen

"We're not going back." - Erin

The walk to her office is no longer the act of a new attorney marking territory, but the measured steps of a condemned woman rehearsing the route to the gallows. Each footfall on the commercial carpet is absorbed by the building's engineered silence, but Erin imagines the sound carries, through glass, through breakrooms, through the quiet calculus of colleagues already placing bets.

The firm's oxygen is different now. Charged. Every molecule slightly misaligned.

Associates pretend to work. Screens glow. Fingers move. But attention gathers around her in fragments, half-glances, delayed reactions, the faint tightening of posture as she passes. Not hostility. Something worse. Curiosity. Rumors.

How long will she last?

Erin keys into her office, the click of the lock louder than it should be. She doesn't remove her coat. The Harper file lands on her desk like evidence; clean, closed, but still contaminated.

Her phone vibrates.

Radcliffe. 10:00 sharp.

No subject.

A summons.

Radcliffe's office sits at the end of the corridor like a final checkpoint. Glass walls. City behind him. No place to hide.

He doesn't stand.

"Ms. Carter. Sit."

She does.

He studies her for a moment, pen balanced between his fingers.

"I've had better mornings," he says. "Let's talk about the Harper case."

No accusation. No softness either.

"The husband's counsel reached out," he continues. "Used the word *fraternizing*."

A pause.

"Optics are poor. Exposure is worse. This isn't about guilt. It's about liability."

Erin nods. "Understood."

Radcliffe leans forward slightly.

"I'm going to ask you one question. I expect a direct answer."

A beat.

"Is there anything, anything at all, that could come out of this that puts this firm at risk?"

Erin doesn't know how much he knows and for a fraction of a second, she considers telling him everything.

Instead:

"No, sir."

Silence stretches.

Then—

"That's all I needed."

He makes a note, almost absently.

"The divorce was withdrawn. No complaint filed. No Bar issue. No HR escalation."

The words land clean. Controlled.

Radcliffe finally looks up again.

"Whatever you did," he says, almost conversational, "it worked."

A pause.

"I don't recommend making a habit of it."

Erin says nothing.

"You're still here because you're good," he continues. "Better than most first-years we've seen."

Another pause.

"But you're on notice."

He sets the pen down.

"You don't get another misstep."

Erin nods. "I understand."

Radcliffe leans back.

"Social services sent over a case after our discussion about you this morning. I happen to know the director over there. I'm assigning you to it."

A folder slides across the desk.

CARTER, JAMIE – CUSTODY PETITION

Erin's fingers still on it.

"No drama this time," he adds. "Play it straight. I think you'll want to get this done the traditional way."

"Yes, sir."

She stands.

"And Ms. Carter—"

She turns.

"That was a gutsy move."

A flicker of something—approval, maybe.

Then:

"Don't do it again."

Back in her office, the air feels different.

Not safe. But hers.

She sits. Opens the new file.

She reads. No narrative. No rescue.

Just facts.

This isn't redemption. But it is survival.

And now—

It's a case.

The file is thin.

Too thin.

Attendance reports. Incomplete.

Nutritional concerns, suggested, not confirmed.

Prior notes. Observations. Nothing decisive.

Erin flips through it again, slower this time.

There's no single event. No incident that forces action.

Just pattern.

And pattern doesn't argue. It accumulates.

Her phone buzzes once.

A forwarded report. School system.

Three absences. Same week.

She exhales.

Now it's moving.

The house smells the same.

Oil. Smoke. Something stale beneath it.

Dan stands slightly ahead of her at the door, clipboard in hand. He knocks once. Firm. Professional.

The door opens.

Mr. Carter.

Recognition flickers. Then hardens.

"You again."

Dan doesn't react. He notices Mr. Carter glaring at Erin without speaking.

"Just a follow-up," he says evenly. "Routine."

They step inside.

Everything is arranged. Clean enough. Ordered enough.

Performative.

Erin says nothing. She watches.

Mrs. Carter appears from the kitchen, already smiling.

"Everything's fine," she says too quickly.

Dan nods, making a note.

"Jamie home?"

"He's studying."

"Let's check in anyway."

Jamie sits on the couch when they enter.

Still. Too still.

He looks at Dan. Then at Erin.

Then down.

Dan asks the usual questions. School. Sleep. Meals.

Answers come short. Controlled.

"Yes."

"Fine."

"Normal."

Then—

A pause.

Dan waits.

Jamie shrugs.

"Sometimes we eat later."

It's nothing.

And it's everything.

Dan writes it down. Erin doesn't move.

Outside, on the walkway, Dan closes the folder.

"If you're filing," he says without looking at her, "file it right."

She nods.

"Half-cases don't work."

Then he walks away.

No reassurance.

No alliance.

Just the truth.

The evidence builds slowly.

Not dramatically. But steadily.

Erin assembles:

Attendance patterns. Medical gaps. Financial records; irregular, unstable.

Dan's reports arrive through official channels. Nothing more. Nothing less.

No strategy discussions.

No coordination.

Just documentation putting together evidence that has been building over time.

Erin organizes everything. Color-coded. Indexed. Timelined. Not to impress. To prove.

It's not one thing.

It's never one thing.

It's the pattern.

Family court is smaller than expected.

Fluorescent lighting. Worn carpet. No grandeur.

Just process.

Jamie sits at the table, feet barely touching the floor.

He answers questions simply.

No embellishment.

No performance.

"Sometimes they forget to pick me up."

"I walk home when they don't come get me."

"Food is locked."

"They yell a lot."

"Sometimes mom doesn't wake up."

"Dad passes out on the couch."

Silence follows each answer.

Heavy.

Unavoidable.

The parents' attorney tries to redirect.

Birthdays. Holidays.

"Didn't you get a bike?"

Jamie nods.

"It didn't work. Dad beat it with a bat."

Erin asks one question.

"Do you feel safe at home?"

Jamie thinks.

Then:

"No."

That's enough.

The judge reviews the file in silence.

Pages turn. Notes made.

No drama.

No delay.

Then:

"The Court finds the current environment is not safe for the minor."

A pause.

"Custody is transferred to the petitioner. Effective immediately."

No one reacts at first.

Then—

A breath.

A shift.

Something final.

Jamie looks at Erin.

"Does that mean I get to go with you?"

She nods, but her throat tightens before the word comes.

"Yes."

He doesn't react right away. Just looks at her, like he's waiting for it to be taken back.

Then, slowly, the tension leaves his face.

It isn't a big smile. Not loud. Not practiced.

Just something small and real.

And it hits her harder than anything else has.

Outside the courthouse, the air feels different.

Not lighter.

Just open.

Jamie walks beside her, backpack slung over one shoulder.

No rush.

No fear.

Just movement.

"Where to?" he asks.

Erin looks ahead.

Anywhere.

Everywhere.

"This time," she says quietly, "we're not going back."

He nods.

And keeps walking.

This time, she didn't have to run.

She just had to stay.

Epilogue

"There are no coincidences. Only moments we don't understand yet." - Erin

Morning comes quietly now.

Not the violent kind that drags the day in behind it, but something softer, light easing through the blinds in narrow bands, settling across the kitchen table in a way that feels almost intentional. The apartment still carries the unfamiliar weight of stability. No slammed doors. No raised voices bleeding through drywall. Just the low, ordinary sounds of a life that no longer has to brace for impact.

Erin stands at the counter, one hand wrapped around a mug that has long since cooled. She hasn't moved in a while. The stillness is new to her. It feels less like rest and more like something earned, something she doesn't quite trust yet.

Behind her, a chair scrapes lightly against the floor.

Jamie.

He moves through the kitchen without asking permission, without checking the air first. That, more than anything, is how she knows things are different. He opens the fridge, studies its contents with exaggerated seriousness, then shuts it again like a man who has options.

"You ever gonna eat," he says, glancing at her over his shoulder, "or are you just gonna stare at coffee until it files a complaint?"

She exhales something that almost resembles a laugh.

"Working on it."

He nods, satisfied, then drops into the chair across from her. For a moment, neither of them says anything. They don't need to. The silence isn't empty anymore. It doesn't demand to be filled.

It just is.

Jamie leans back, balancing the chair on two legs, testing the boundaries of a world that no longer punishes him for small risks. His gaze drifts toward the window, toward the ordinary street below, cars passing, people moving, nothing remarkable.

"Still feels weird," he says.

"What does?"

"This." He gestures vaguely around the room. "Not having to… you know."

She does know.

She nods. "Yeah."

He studies her for a second, like he's about to say something more, then thinks better of it. Or maybe just decides it doesn't need to be said. He lets the chair fall forward again with a soft thud.

Across the table, Erin watches him, not the way she used to, cataloging damage, anticipating impact, but simply watching. Taking inventory of something that no longer needs to be hidden.

He catches her looking.

"What?"

"Nothing."

"You're doing that thing."

"What thing?"

"Where you act like everything's fine but you're thinking about something else."

She considers denying it.

Doesn't.

"Just thinking," she says.

"Dangerous."

"Usually."

He smirks; easy, unguarded and reaches for a piece of toast, tearing it in half without ceremony.

For a moment, she lets herself stay there. In the ordinary. In the quiet.

And then, like a thread pulled from somewhere deeper, the memory returns.

Her grandmother's voice.

Not loud. Never loud. Just certain.

There are no coincidences. Only moments we don't understand yet.

Erin shifts her gaze to the window, to the reflection faintly overlaying the street beyond. For a second, she sees both versions of herself there, the one who built this life, and the one who survived long enough to reach it.

She thinks about the hotel room.

The booking that wasn't supposed to matter.

The man who didn't want anything.

The conversation that should have ended there.

But didn't.

She thinks about how easily it could have gone another way. A different client. A different night. A different choice.

None of this.

No Jamie at the table.

No quiet.

No second chance at anything.

And yet—

here it is.

Not clean. Not perfect. But real.

She doesn't try to name it. Doesn't try to turn it into something larger than it needs to be.

But for the first time, she allows the possibility that it wasn't random.

That maybe some intersections don't happen by accident.

That sometimes the thing that looks like chaos is just a pattern you can't see yet.

Behind her, Jamie stands, grabbing his jacket off the chair.

"I'm heading out," he says. "Don't do anything illegal while I'm gone."

"No promises."

He grins, already halfway to the door.

"Seriously. You're like one bad decision away from being a case study."

"Go to school."

"I am."

He pauses at the door, hand on the knob, then looks back at her, just for a second.

Not checking.

Not asking.

Just… looking.

Then he nods, once, and disappears into the hallway.

The door closes.

The apartment settles again into its quiet rhythm.

Erin stands there a moment longer, the cooled coffee still in her hand, the light shifting slowly across the floor.

She takes a breath.

And this time—

it doesn't feel like she's waiting for something to go wrong.

A Note from the Author

This is a love story though not the kind we are often told.

It is a story about survival, about the hidden weight people carry, and about the quiet ways trauma shapes the paths we walk.

Erin's story is not meant to be judged too quickly. Like many lives, it is more complicated than it first appears.

It is also a story about the different forms love can take—
the kind that protects,
the kind that endures,
and the kind that offers a way forward when all seems lost.

This book is for those who have endured, who have been misunderstood, and who still believe that something good can come from even the most difficult roads.

Thank you for reading.
— Carol Martin

About the Author

Carol Martin writes intelligent fiction for readers who value depth, moral tension, and emotional realism. Her stories explore love and consequence in a modern world, where strength is earned, desire has weight, and redemption is possible.

www.ingramcontent.com/pod-product-compliance
Lightning Source LLC
LaVergne TN
LVHW051002080826
845145LV00009B/2423

* 9 7 8 0 9 7 4 7 1 0 8 5 3 *